D1439049

Fergus is a multi-award-winning actor, comedian and writer for television. *Murder at Crime Manor* is his second novel. He lives 198 miles east of Exeter.

# MURDER AT CRIME MANOR

## FERGUS CRAIG

SPHERE

SPHERE

First published in Great Britain in 2022 by Sphere

1 3 5 7 9 10 8 6 4 2

A CIP catalogue record for this book
is available from the British Library.

Hardback ISBN 978-1-4087-2733-1

Typeset in Caslon by M Rules
Printed and bound in Great Britain by
Clays Ltd, Elcograf S.p.A.

Papers used by Sphere are from well-managed forests
and other responsible sources.

Sphere
An imprint of
Little, Brown Book Group
Carmelite House
50 Victoria Embankment
London EC4Y 0DZ

An Hachette UK Company
www.hachette.co.uk

www.littlebrown.co.uk

*Dedicated to the many thousands of people murdered
in isolated British manor houses every year.*

# AUTHOR'S NOTE

Game show hosts aside, the publishing industry is a difficult place to make serious money. That is why, with this book, I made the difficult decision to enter the area of product placement. I have personally contacted a number of companies and although, at the time of writing, I am yet to receive a reply, I am confident that a high six-figure deal will be forthcoming. With that in mind, I have made a few discreet references to leading brand names in the book. I think it works well and, I hope, doesn't distract from your enjoyment of the novel.

# PROLOGUE

Cold. So cold. As cold as a KitKat Chunky sitting in a refrigerator. As cold as a refreshing bottle of Heineken on a hot summer's day. As cold as snow. Because it was snow, although Detective Roger LeCarre didn't know that yet because he was slowly regaining consciousness.

His handsome face felt as if it was going through some kind of unnecessarily vigorous spa treatment. But this couldn't be a spa treatment because Detective Roger LeCarre didn't go for spa treatments. His idea of skincare was a fist fight in which both parties agreed to 'stay away from the face'. If you handed Roger LeCarre a gift token for a spa treatment he'd throw it into a nearby furnace or more realistically just say 'thank you' and then give it to his wife Carrie.

No. This was no spa treatment. This was something else.

The sharp, cold pain on his face was nothing compared to the dull, throbbing pain on the back of his head.

He had to move. Something told him there was more pain coming.

Some people liked pain. Sickos. When LeCarre worked vice, he'd find some otherwise respectable accountant in some Bodmin brothel humiliating themselves and paying for the privilege. He'd handcuff them and read them their rights, pants still around their ankles. They probably liked it. More humiliation. *Sickos.* One Valentine's Day he and Carrie had got curious and tried it out for themselves. Carrie spanking him, digging her heels into his back, squeezing and tugging his southerly region with implements that had arrived in the post that morning in a discreet package from LoveHoney.com.

'Can we stop this, please? It is literally the opposite of pleasurable.'

'I thought you wanted to try something new,' Carrie had said.

'Yeah, well, I've changed my mind. I think I just like normal sex. Passionate, athletic but broadly normal sex.'

This wasn't sex. This was anything but. This was Detective Roger LeCarre coming to the realisation that he was face down in snow with a serious blow to the back of his head.

*They wanted him dead.*

He hadn't noticed his handsome ears ringing until now. There was another noise too. Footsteps. Rapid, frantic, heavy footsteps pounding through the snow. Getting louder. Getting closer.

They wanted to finish the job.

(By which I mean killing Detective Roger LeCarre.)

# ONE

Detective Roger LeCarre made his way through the Devon countryside with the satisfaction of a man who'd wisely fitted his Kia Ceed with winter tyres. The man at Halfords had said all-weather tyres should do the trick in British conditions. The wreckage by the side of the road said the man at Halfords was wrong.

Should LeCarre have stopped and offered the two fresh-faced constables assistance? A nasty crash like that could do with a senior officer on the scene. No. They'd have to learn someday. Much as he'd like to, Detective Roger LeCarre couldn't police Devon and Cornwall all by himself. Besides, he was supposed to be off duty.

*Off duty.*

LeCarre let out a large manly chuckle at the thought.

There was no such thing. Not for him. Ever since the day he'd first put on the uniform, he'd been on duty. Crime didn't sleep, so neither did he. Obviously, technically, he *did* sleep, science dictated that he had to, but his duty didn't sleep. If he saw crime, he dealt with it. Whether he was on Devon and Cornwall police time or not.

LeCarre often made arrests in his dreams. Last night he'd arrested a horse for robbing a Budgens. Clearly, the whole incident was a slumbering figment but in LeCarre's book, it still counted as an arrest and when he'd awoken, he'd added it to his tally.

The snow fell down like white droplets of cold, fluffy rain. Like snow. Devon hadn't seen snow like this for a long time, not since the year LeCarre joined the force. A very long time indeed. He still remembered his first arrest. Heck, the whole force did. It was snowing that day. Most officers make their first arrest with a traffic offence, or a burglary. A 'petty crime'. LeCarre hated the term. An oxymoron. How could crime be petty? It was crime!

*His* first arrest? An obscure and ancient bylaw said that it was illegal to eat duck inside Exeter's city walls on a Monday. Four hundred years the law had been there, never used. There was no record of anyone being arrested for such a crime. It was just one of those old

6

laws, an oddity to be read out as entertaining trivia on breakfast radio.

That was, until PC Roger LeCarre came along. His fellow officers couldn't believe it when he leaped across the table in a Harvester restaurant, pinning an unsuspecting diner against the wall.

'You're under arrest under the Poultry Act of 1674.'

The law was the law. LeCarre had read it and now he was here to uphold it.

That was his first arrest. His last arrest was this morning. How many had there been in between? Thousands. Tens of thousands? Probably. Thieves, fraudsters, fighters, beaters, speeders, drinkers, druggers ... *murderers*. They'd all made their way to LeCarre's door at one time or another and they'd all had to pay the toll. What was the toll?

*Time*.

That morning, LeCarre had been strolling through an M&S Food feeling a deep sense of national pride as he admired its classy yet affordable selection of cold meats. Suddenly, sensing something, he'd tilted his nose to the air and inhaled – *crime*. Quickly, he'd turned to see a schoolgirl illegally placing a 170 gram packet of Percy Pigs in her coat pocket.

'Put down the pigs or I shoot!' LeCarre's hand had hovered over his taser.

The girl had frozen, neatly syncing with the cabinet of party food behind her.

'The only pig in this place is you, copper.'

LeCarre had thrown her into a stack of Colin the Caterpillar birthday cakes. The Colins' chocolate eyes seemed to express somehow the dark mood that had descended upon the place.

'You want 50,000 volts running through ya? Well, do ya? Do ya?'

The girl had meekly shaken her criminal head. This little piggy was in LeCarre's world now and she was a fish out of water.

'In my office, LeCarre. Now!' Chief Superintendent Beverley Chang said, as soon as the girl was charged and on her way to a young offenders unit.

'Happy New Year, Detective.' The words exited LeCarre's boss's luscious lips with a deep, sensual sincerity. LeCarre knew those lips. He knew them only too well.

'Happy New Year, ma'am.'

'Any New Year's resolutions, Detective?'

'Same as every year, ma'am. To stop crime wherever I find it. And also to start remembering to leave the house with a carrier bag to avoid the ridiculous 10p charge.'

'You can't arrest everyone, you know, LeCarre,' Chang said.

'Sounds like a challenge.'

'I'm serious, LeCarre. Devon and Cornwall's prison service doesn't have enough capacity for a copper with your . . . ' she searched for the right word, 'appetite.'

'Guess they need to build some more prisons.'

'We police by consent. If you arrest the whole two counties, there'll be no one left to consent. Just a land of police officers, with nothing to do.'

'Sounds pretty good to me. Perhaps I could finally learn an instrument,' LeCarre said, with typically excellent humour.

'How would you learn it, Roger? All the teachers would be in prison.'

'YouTube?'

LeCarre wasn't willing to concede it, but Chang had a point.

'I've had an invitation for you.' Chang took a golden envelope from her desk drawer. 'I'd like you to accept.'

Chang leaned over to hand it to him, her considerable cleavage showing. He and that cleavage had history, but that's just what it was – *history.* Like the Stuarts and the Tudors, the Boer War, the Ottoman Empire. Whatever had happened between Detective Roger LeCarre and the body of Chief Superintendent Beverley Chang was in the past. Like the French Revolution or the invention of gravity, LeCarre had no truck with it now. Looking at that cleavage was like looking at a Simon Schama programme about the Edwardian age, although this was the sexiest Simon Schama programme he'd ever seen.

LeCarre's gaze turned to the golden envelope now resting in his hand. An invitation? Detective Roger LeCarre didn't much like the word. When he received an invitation it was usually to 'step outside', but those kind of invitations didn't come in golden envelopes, they came in Plymouth accents, delivered by testosterone-sodden men in football shirts.

*This looked like an invitation worth opening.*

He delicately set the card inside free from its paper casing, which is to say, he took it out of the envelope.

*Eli Jefferson Quartz, the 23rd Earl of Devon, warmly invites Detective Roger LeCarre to Powderham Castle on the evening of Friday, 6 January to celebrate the Earl's accession to the title. 7 p.m. Black tie. The Earl plans to celebrate in style. All guests will be provided with an en suite room for the night, followed by a magnificent breakfast.*

LeCarre's gaze hit Chang's, just as she had clearly anticipated.

'Ma'am.'

'Not your scene?'

'Not exactly, no.'

LeCarre's intellect belonged in rarified climes, but he'd always felt more at home with the salt of the earth in the Crown and Goose, which although under new management and with some worrying steps into the realm of 'craft beer', still retained its status as LeCarre's favourite pub in Exeter.

'I take it you haven't heard of Mr Quartz?' Chang said.

'The name is familiar. I'm a police officer; the closest I get to royalty is a drugs bust in a Greene King pub or a pub called the Rose and Crown or the Queen's Head or maybe the King's Arms or the Prince of Wales or the Duke of Edinburgh or something like that. Basically a drugs bust in a pub with a royal name, do you see what I'm getting at?'

'I do,' said Chang.

'Like a Prince Albert or a Duke of York,' said LeCarre.

'I get the point,' said Chang.

'Not sure I've done one in a while, actually. I think I did a drugs bust in a Red Lion last year, but that's not a royal name, so . . . ' Roger LeCarre paused for a moment. 'Sorry, what were we talking about?'

'Eli Quartz,' said Chang.

'Prince William in Dawlish! Sorry, I'm just trying to think of pubs with royal names now. That's it. Done. Eli . . . *Quartz*? Tell me about him.'

Chang leaned back in her chair and steepled her fingers together, like the high-powered woman she was.

'As the invitation says, Eli Quartz is the new Earl of Devon,' she said, 'but there's something about Mr Quartz that's very different from the twenty-two Earls of Devon that came before him . . . he's American.'

An *American* Earl of Devon. She might as well have told him there was a canine pope.

'Wh-wh – what?' LeCarre stuttered. 'How?'

'He purchased the title.'

'Can you do such a thing?' asked LeCarre.

'For the right price, it would seem so,' said Chang. 'And, rumour has it, Mr Quartz paid a very high price indeed.'

'What's this got to do with Detective Roger LeCarre?' said Detective Roger LeCarre, referring to himself in the third person. 'It's not illegal, I presume?'

'Not illegal, no. Concerning? Perhaps. Eli Quartz is a multi-billionaire and a very powerful man. He's chosen to make our humble county his new home and in rather a grand way. I think it's important that the Devon and

Cornwall police force have a good relationship with such an individual, don't you?'

'Why me? I'm hardly what you might call a people person. I'm better at arresting people than making friends with them.'

This had been a consistent problem in LeCarre's life. He'd meet someone, they'd start to become friends, and then one day they'd commit some obscure minor offence like defacing the Queen by folding a bank note and LeCarre would arrest them.

'Can't you send someone else?'

'Believe me, if I could, I would. I was rather keen on going myself. A weekend at the castle of an attractive bachelor billionaire sounds . . . ' Chang licked her powerful lips erotically but also a bit weirdly, 'delightful. Unfortunately for me, Quartz's people were very insistent. The invitation was for one man and one man only.'

LeCarre knew that man better than perhaps anyone else on Earth, and yet in many ways he hardly knew him at all. Because that man was a fascinating enigma, a complex character, capable of carrying a series of books and, if the money was right, a TV series probably best suited to the Sunday evening 9 p.m. slot on BBC1 or ITV.

Because that man was him.

*Because that man was Detective Roger LeCarre.*

# TWO

Detective Roger LeCarre's Kia Ceed pulled up to the giant iron gates. They looked like the gates to another world. One day he might pull his Kia Ceed up to the Pearly Gates. Not today, he hoped. In fact, with luck, that day would come so far in the future that he'd be driving a car that hadn't yet been invented, or maybe even some kind of jet pack.

These gates didn't lead to heaven, but their grandeur suggested a world no less luxurious. Through the snow, he could make out the gold-plated letters 'PC'.

Powderham Castle.

LeCarre pondered on what to do. He didn't know the procedure. He was a man far more used to entering night-clubs, criminal lairs, women, than he was entering the grounds of ancient estates. Just as he was about to get out of his car to look for some sign of an intercom, the gates opened, revealing a little bridge over a stream and a long driveway leading to the castle itself.

As the pretty sight of Powderham Castle, the fortified manor house and its glorious snow-covered grounds was laid out in front of him, LeCarre allowed a pleasant thought to enter his handsome brain: a brief vacation from crime could be good for him. Out there, beyond this wintery paradise, were Devon and Cornwall, two counties pulsating with ceaseless crime. A world like that made it impossible for a man like Detective Roger LeCarre to relax. Here was a retreat. A place so beautiful that something as ugly as crime simply couldn't penetrate its walls.

The evening ahead was filled with many mysteries. What it held, LeCarre simply did not know. He could be certain of only one thing – no crime would be taking place tonight.

That was for sure.

The castle's long approach gave LeCarre some time to run over the information he'd been able to acquire on Eli Quartz in the brief time since he had left his sexy superior, Chief Superintendent Beverley Chang.

A thirty-six-year-old tech titan, Quartz had made his fortune in California's famous Silicon Valley. What little LeCarre knew of him, he liked. Unlike many of his fellow computer nerds, Quartz was a man who actually made things. Amazon, Google, Facebook, these weren't tangible objects, they were flimsy concepts built on air. When LeCarre's daughter had joined Instagram, he had considered doing the same thing, in the hope of finding a shared interest, but he couldn't work out what it was. That afternoon he'd walked into every shop on Exeter High Street asking if they had any Instagrams in stock, but to no avail. Quartz and his business, Quartz Industries, made things – real things. Watches, cars, robots. This was something LeCarre could get on board with. Perhaps he'd even be lucky enough to leave with a goody bag containing a 'smart pen' or something.

Two key questions hung in the air like Quartz-made drones: why had Eli Quartz crossed the Atlantic Ocean to settle in East Devon? And why had he been so insistent that Detective Roger LeCarre should attend his lavish castle-warming?

A small collection of cars was parked in front of the castle's entrance. A quick assessment suggested not all of LeCarre's fellow attendees had the limits of a Devon and Cornwall police salary. He parked beside a luxury Tesla. LeCarre had no time for electric vehicles. If God had intended cars to be powered by electricity then he'd have made them that way. LeCarre shuddered at the thought that he might be about to spend an evening amongst the liberal metropolitan elite, the 'woke'. LeCarre was woke: long hours and a serious Red Bull habit meant that he was woke most of the time, but he didn't feel the need to bang on about it.

LeCarre exited his Kia Ceed and looked at his reflection in the driver's side window. His tuxedo still fitted nicely. Good. A few years had passed since that night. LeCarre lived on a man's diet of pasties, booze and KitKat Chunkies, but the life of a Devon and Cornwall police officer kept him in shape. Nothing burned calories like the battle against crime. Carrie had tried to get him onto what she called a 'balanced diet'. 'You can't chase down a suspect with kale in your belly, Carrie. You just can't,' he'd protested. She had no complaints about his body in the bedroom: he had, in his opinion, for a man in his age bracket, one of the top 250 most attractive top halves in East Devon.

The tuxedo hadn't been worn since he and Carrie had gone to a fancy-dress party and Roger had chosen to dress as James Bond. That was a good night. He hadn't wanted to go to the party. 'Fancy dress is for children, Carrie. It's for *children*.' As the evening went on he'd grown into the role, drinking vodka martinis, doing a Sean Connery voice and, just before they went home, punching a foreign man for no particular reason.

Eli Quartz's invitation had suggested guests bring an overnight bag. LeCarre worried the rucksack on his back didn't quite go with the tuxedo. Imagine it's a parachute, he said to himself and instantly felt cool again.

LeCarre stood in front of the castle's six-hundred-year-old Gothic façade. They say an Englishman's home is his castle but LeCarre had never liked that phrase because, in the vast majority of cases, an Englishman's home is his house. Most Englishmen didn't have castles. In this particular instance, it was an American whose home was his castle, and a very nice home it was too.

No greeting party. No signs of a celebration, already begun. Just a large, pointed arch, with a red, wooden door. He checked himself for signs of nerves but found none. Detective Roger LeCarre was used to walking through doors not knowing what was behind them. Usually, it was a case of hookers, junkies, dead bodies, or sometimes just a disabled toilet. Whatever lay behind this door would make a pleasant change. He straightened his dinner jacket and stepped up to the entrance, pressing the doorbell. It had never occurred to him that castles had doorbells. Underneath the pageantry, I guess we're all the same, he said to himself in an incredibly deep and meaningful way. In another life, LeCarre could have had a column in a leading national newspaper, such was his capacity for philosophical thought.

Ding. Dong. Footsteps. The door opened.

'Hello, I'm ...'

'Detective Roger LeCarre. We're delighted you were able to join us. Please, come inside. You must be cold.'

The man who'd come to greet him, the butler, he supposed, was a mass of sturdy, upright Englishness. A bald head with trim grey hair at the back and sides. His frame was large, not with fat, but not with muscle either. With something else. Like an old oak tree who'd inexplicably developed an ability to walk and talk. On the bridge of his nose rested a pair of round glasses. His chin was weak, but not his demeanour. The man looked like he was born in another century, which being at least sixty years of age, he obviously was. But perhaps another century altogether, another era. This man, who presumably worked for Eli Quartz, a man who represented the future, seemed to come from the past. It was impossible to picture him using an iPad, for example, but very easy to see him operating a mangle. He looked like a snooker referee but not one of the women ones they seem so keen on having nowadays, thought LeCarre.

'I hope I'm not too early. The invitation said 7 p.m.,' said LeCarre, stepping inside, brushing the snow from his suit.

'Not at all, sir.'

LeCarre looked to the enormous grandfather clock that stood behind the butler. Twenty-five minutes past six. He liked to be punctual.

'I'm glad you're here, Detective LeCarre. We've all so been looking forward to meeting you.'

Just then, a beautiful servant girl in her twenties shyly approached, her voluptuous eyes flitting between LeCarre and the marble floor. Again, the young woman seemed not of this time. It was like these two people belonged to the castle and not the outside world. Like they'd been there the six hundred years since it was built, like they came with the package. That said, LeCarre recognised her scent as Flame by Britney Spears so it was fair to assume she either popped into Exeter town centre from time to time or ordered the perfume online.

'This is Angela,' said the butler. 'She'll show you to your room.'

'Can I take your bag for you, Detective LeCarre?'

'No, no,' said LeCarre. Although uncomfortable with the idea, LeCarre was prepared to take on the role of waited-upon guest, but he drew the line at a woman carrying his bag. The only exception was if he had, for some reason, two dodgy wrists. That exact circumstance actually happened after a ten-pin bowling accident in his late thirties, after which Carrie had had to carry everything for him for six months while his wrists were allowed to heal. 'I'm hating this more than you, Carrie, I really am,' he'd said, as she carried his bag to and from the car every day.

The young lady he now knew as Angela really was a delight to look at, like a professional oil painting or an Audi S5. LeCarre was reluctant to call anything perfect – he made a point of never giving higher than a four-star review on Amazon because there's always room for improvement – but her beauty was the closest he'd got to awarding something five stars since the brilliantly effective Waterpik water flosser he'd purchased last spring.

He searched Angela for an imperfection but couldn't find one. Her two long arms hung beautifully from her shoulders in perfect proportion. Her blonde hair fell down from her head covering what he supposed must be a truly stunning pair of ears. Angela's long neck served as an elegant plinth for her exquisite head, which contained high cheekbones which lay on her face like two tiny camel humps either side of Devon's most delightful nose. Her eyes. *Her* eyes. What colour were they? They weren't blue, no. Nor brown, nor green. What was it? If only he had a Dulux swatch wheel with him to try and figure it out. It was like a new colour, one LeCarre had never seen before. Her feminine jaw led to a chin featuring a single charming dimple large enough to store one average-sized currant. Put all that together and you had the recipe for a face more delicious than any Michelin-starred meal. Also, she had quite nice breasts.

'Please, follow me,' said Angela, turning to reveal the reverse side of a slender figure unrestrained in its capacity to impress by the dowdy grey servant's uniform in which it hid. And to think that a mouth belonging to that body was inviting LeCarre to follow it to a bedroom.

Ping.

A text from LeCarre's wife.

*Have a good time at the party. Can I delete your* Dragon's Den *episodes from the Sky planner? We're down to 3 per cent.*

*No. I'm still planning on watching them*, LeCarre quickly replied, following Angela up a winding set of stairs.

# THREE

Detective Roger LeCarre sat on the edge of the king-size four-poster bed. He was alone. Just as well, he thought. He gave himself a mental pat on the back for not having sex with Angela. LeCarre, he often said, was his own worst critic, but it was important to give himself credit when he did something particularly good like not betraying his wife with a beautiful servant girl in a castle.

Angela had told him that he had some time to relax before a drinks reception in the music room downstairs, so he took a moment to take in his temporary sleeping chamber. The bedroom he'd been given for the night was unlike any he'd ever been in. LeCarre thought his own bedroom was lavish. He and Carrie had refurbished it in the Jury's Inn style they'd grown so fond of, complete with mini fridge, writing desk and trouser press. As an expression of Roger and Carrie's shared love of travel, they'd made an exact replica. A safe, a tray with a kettle, tea bags, UHT milk on it, a hair dryer in a little bag in a drawer. They'd even gone so far as to install a hermetically sealed window to give it that real holiday feel. But this bedroom? This was something else.

The gold-framed bed was surrounded on all sides by red velvet curtains with golden trim and elaborate tassels. Who had slept in this bed before him? Kings? Queens? Maybe Romesh Ranganathan in a travel documentary? The walls were coated with gold embossed wallpaper so expertly applied that LeCarre expected a steam roller had been used to do the job.

Despite the freezing cold weather outside, the room was warm due to a raging fire which thankfully was deliberate and contained within a fireplace. On the floor was a rug made from a real polar bear, its head still intact. The room contained a number of paintings, the most striking of which hung directly above the fireplace: a handsome man, sitting proudly upon a horse, dressed in what LeCarre presumed was the military dress of his time. What time that was, LeCarre couldn't tell. Certainly the picture was from some time in what LeCarre referred broadly to as 'the olden days', pre the invention of fridge-freezers.

How would LeCarre have fared in such an era? Well, he'd like to think. Yes, he'd miss the comforts of the twenty-first century – shower gel, smart phones, his Waterpik water flosser – but 'the olden days' were a time when men could be men and LeCarre was, if nothing else, a man. Now, apparently, men were expected to do womanly things like change nappies. Though he was careful where he said it, that sort of thing didn't sit well with Detective Roger LeCarre. For a start, he didn't have easy access to a baby so where was he supposed to find a nappy to change? This man – this man on the horse – no one expected him to change nappies. Nappies didn't even exist in his era, probably – babies were just expected to excrete into their clothes as nature intended.

LeCarre looked into the man's eyes and felt a connection through the centuries. They were, it felt to him, men of the same mind in some way. The man seemed to be looking at LeCarre but also out over the land, his land. Did this man once own Devon? LeCarre felt that in many ways he owned Devon now, although technically he only owned 1,200 square feet of it in the shape of his three-bedroomed semi-detached, and at least 60 per cent of that was to all intents and purposes owned by the Coventry Building Society.

LeCarre didn't know the artist, but to his untrained eye this looked like an excellent painting. He'd heard it said that with the truly great paintings, the subject's eyes followed you around the room. He decided to test the theory by hopping around the bedroom and looking back at the picture. The eyes did indeed seem to follow him everywhere. This was a truly great painting and this really was a truly great bedroom.

The wind outside howled like some kind of loud wolf. LeCarre walked over to the window and pulled aside the heavy gold curtain. The snow continued to fall at a rapid rate. His Kia Ceed was already half buried. Some storm this was. LeCarre had never seen anything quite like it. At least it was cars that would be buried tonight and not people. LeCarre had seen too many people buried. Three murders in Exeter already this year and some people hadn't even taken down their Christmas trees yet. Nope, there'd be no murders tonight. *Of that he could be absolutely, positively sure.*

LeCarre looked at his expensive waterproof watch. Still some time before the drinks reception. He slipped off his brown brogues (which, if he was honest with himself, didn't really go with the tuxedo and were probably the reason he'd missed out on a prize at the fancy-dress party where he'd gone as James Bond) and climbed into bed.

For the first time since his wedding night, he stared up at the underside of the roof of a four-poster bed frame. He spotted a small tear in the fabric. Not everything in this room was perfect. Perhaps not everything was as it seemed. Who were the other guests? Nobody had told him. Was LeCarre being naive? He usually liked to know something of a venue before entering – who was there? Were there any weapons? Where were the exits? How was the wifi?

Since arriving at the castle he'd mentally clocked off duty. That wasn't like him. The magnificence of the building, the magnificence of Angela, had thrown him somehow. He checked himself. *Always be ready for anything, within reason.* That was his personal motto. It was important to remind himself of it now.

Tonight was a gathering of people. People of high status, no doubt, but people all the same, and if life had taught Detective Roger LeCarre anything it was that wherever people gathered, *crime* came.

Just then, LeCarre turned his head and noticed a picture on the bedside table, a modern picture, a photograph of a young man. LeCarre did a double take, which is actually quite hard to do when you're lying down. Why the double take? *Because it was a man he recognised.*

# FOUR

Detective Roger LeCarre heard the gentle hum of party chit-chat already underway in the music room as he came down the stairs, although 'party' seemed like an over-statement. It only sounded like two people. LeCarre had imagined at least a hundred. He adjusted his expectations. If this was an intimate affair then how had he found his way onto the guest list? Maybe the force was finally getting the respect it deserved. He chuckled at the thought. Chance would be a fine thing.

LeCarre felt a strange unease. Not too late to make an exit, he thought. If I leave now, I could be home in time for *Question of Sport*. LeCarre wasn't sure about the new revamped line-up and despaired at a nation that only truly appreciated Sue Barker when she was no longer there, but he was a loyal viewer all the same. *Question of Sport* was still the home of quality sports-based banter, something he feared he wouldn't find in the castle tonight.

That face, the one from the photograph on the bedside table, the picture of the man, at the end of the last chapter, the one he recognised – it was on his mind. Where did he know that face from? Every day brought so many new faces, a constant parade of victims and perps, perps and victims, and also the odd shop assistant. It was difficult to keep track. But something about that particular face had stuck with him and yet he couldn't place it. Why was it sitting in an ancient bed chamber in Powderham Castle?

LeCarre's famously piercing blue eyes were met with more new faces as he hesitantly entered the music room. What was that feeling in his belly? Nerves? Entering a crack den – not a problem. Entering a party full of presumably law-abiding civvies – this was unfamiliar territory. The music room gloriously maintained the glamour of another age. The first thing you spotted was the colour – walls of magnificent blueish green. If Carrie suggested such a colour, Roger would enact an immediate veto but here, in Powderham Castle, it somehow worked. The high ceiling was graced with an impressive windowed dome which, were it not January, would be letting in the early evening sunlight. Instead, light came from a gold chandelier and two alabaster lamps as tall as LeCarre. In LeCarre's mind the term 'music room' provoked memories of his childhood school in Totnes. That music room contained only a pathetic box of the kind of percussion instruments he'd never seen used by an actual musician. Bits of wood that you scraped or banged to make some underwhelming sound impossible to call music. Music rooms in castles were different. This contained a grand piano worthy of its adjective and an old organ, one of those ones with a little keyboard and big golden pipes.

Two guests, a man and a woman, stood by a pillar, drinks in hand. Each gave LeCarre a tentative smile. LeCarre approached and tried to think of an opening line. Something that showcased him as the complex, intelligent, erudite yet tough man he was.

'Very snowy out there, isn't it?' he said.

'Quite. Anthony Little-Hope, pleased to meet you,' said the man, extending a weak hand which LeCarre firmly shook.

'Hello,' said the lady, head tilted downwards, eyes peeking upwards, like Princess Diana in that interview. 'Pleased to meet you. Cynthia Pest.'

Anthony Little-Hope was a man of about fifty. LeCarre

quickly played detective. Well-worn black shoes, a three-piece tan-brown corduroy suit, white soft-collared shirt, top button undone and, keeping him loosely within the bounds of the dress code, a black tie. On his head was a mop of curly auburn hair. His skin was pale, unfamiliar with sunlight. The lining of his jacket betrayed something in his inside pocket. A paperback book. From its size and shape, LeCarre guessed it was most likely a copy of Noam Chomsky's 2006 anti-American polemic *Failed States: The Abuse of Power and the Assault on Democracy.* Little-Hope's eyes were small from excessive reading and his teeth were stained with rolled tobacco, the thumb and forefinger of his left hand with ink. Beyond the ink, it was clear to see that his hands had lived a life untroubled by manual labour, or even basic DIY aside from flat-pack furniture assembly. His accent was well-educated, but to the trained ear of Detective Roger LeCarre, he was clearly a long-time Devon resident. Putting the whole package together – the left-wing politics, the pen-pushing lifestyle, the corduroy – Little-Hope was, LeCarre deduced, an academic, almost certainly from the Humanities department of Exeter University.

Cynthia Pest sat somewhere in her thirties and stood in a royal blue chiffon gown that neatly hugged her small and scrappy frame. It was obvious from her air that this was not her first party at a castle. Her brown hair was pulled back tightly into a bun, raising her well-plucked eyebrows slightly so that she had a permanent look of surprise. Pearl and diamond earrings hung from her ears like valuable icicles; her face glistened with recently applied make-up. On her feet was footwear in the form of shoes, high-heeled shoes, that thanks to an old investigation into a shoe heist, LeCarre was able to accurately value in excess of a cool £1,000 – each. Her accent was boarding school clipped: Marlborough College, LeCarre suspected. Pest's energy was confident but there was something about her posture, a slump in the shoulders, that suggested a deep insecurity. Her face was slim and angular, like a bag of knitting needles. Her hollow eyes betrayed long-term insomnia and her narrow septum (which is the bit that separates the nostrils) a predilection for cocaine. This classy lady had a class A habit. The expensive tastes, the excessive lifestyle, the insecurities, the comfort in her surroundings: the equation was simple and the answer was easy – Cynthia Pest was a socialite minor royal.

A lifetime of detection meant that LeCarre was able to make both of these assessments at an incredible pace, in under a second, but he wanted his suspicions confirmed.

'Right,' said LeCarre. 'Shall we start with some small talk? What do you both do?'

'I'm a professor, the head of the History department at Exeter University,' said Anthony Little-Hope.

'And yourself?' said LeCarre, turning to Cynthia Pest.

'Well, I'm the Duchess of Totnes but I like to DJ a little on the side.'

Had Pest or Little-Hope possessed LeCarre's powers of perception they'd have spotted, behind his eyes, a small nod of satisfaction.

'I'm Detective Roger LeCarre. Devon and Cornwall Police. A pleasure to meet you both.'

Pest seemed to shuffle a little.

'Do we know what the plan is?' said LeCarre. 'It can't be just us?'

'No, I shouldn't think so,' said Little-Hope. 'To be honest, I really don't know. It's all very peculiar.'

'You don't know Mr Quartz, then, Professor?' said LeCarre.

'Oh, yes, I've met him a couple of times. He's a very impressive man and he has been very generous to the university. Quite the donation.'

'And yourself, your ... *majesty*?'

'Cynthia, please.'

'I'm sure you know Mr Quartz. You are both royals, after all.'

'Yes, but ... how can I put this? Some of us were born so and some of us were not. I've never met the man. I hardly think he's been in England three months.' Fearing she'd come across blunt, Pest corrected herself a little. 'Of course, he's perfectly charming, I'm sure. For an American.'

The message was clear. If there was a mutual respect between royalty, as far as Pest was concerned, Quartz wasn't, at least not yet, in the club.

'Can I offer you a glass of English Champagne, Detective LeCarre?' said the butler, suddenly standing beside them with a tray.

'English Champagne? There's no such thing. I think you'll find it's sparkling wine and yes, thank you,' said LeCarre, taking a glass.

'Wait!' said Pest, draining her flute and picking up another before the butler left.

LeCarre congratulated himself on avoiding a scene with a protracted conversation about protected designation of origin laws. Last year alone, he'd closed down twenty-five Devon pasty shops for incorrectly calling their pasties Cornish. He'd let the butler off this minor infringement, but it was a helpful reminder that crime was around every corner.

'Um ... sir?' said Little-Hope, after the retreating butler.

'Yes, Mr Little-Hope. My name, should you require it, is Peacock. Arthur Peacock.'

'Ah, Peacock. Pleased to meet you. Do you know when the rest of the guests will be arriving?' said Little-Hope.

'Very soon, I'm sure. Please, help yourself to hors d'oeuvres.'

And there was Angela, the beautiful servant girl, holding a tray of the finest hors d'oeuvres Detective Roger LeCarre had ever seen. He picked up a Waitrose smoked salmon blini and let the delicious concoction melt on his handsome tongue. 'How the other half lives,' he said to himself, in his massive mind. But then his brief journey to taste heaven was disturbed by a commotion from the unlikeliest of sources.

'I will not! I simply will not be treated like this!'

The voice was unmistakable. It came from the famous larynx of Patricia Beresford, glamorous star of BBC Radio Devon's long-running soap opera *Jam on Top*. LeCarre had grown up with it. Anyone with Devon in their blood had. She'd been the voice of the county for years. As Thelma Bertwhistle, the show's feisty central character, Beresford had won Devon hearts long ago. Her turbulent private life provided a steady stream of fodder for the notoriously scandal-hungry West Country press, but she always maintained the respect of her public.

'Is there a problem, Ms Beresford?' asked Peacock, moving towards her with butler-like concern.

'Yes, there most certainly is!' said Patricia Beresford. 'I demand that somebody finds a way to take me home immediately!'

'I'm afraid that won't be possible, madam,' said Peacock.

'Can somebody explain what on earth is going on?' said Professor Anthony Little-Hope, in an attempt to move the plot forward a bit.

'The Bishop, he just told me we're cut off. Stuck here! I say it's ridiculous. Cut off by a bit of snow! I've never heard such absurdity in all my life, and I've been in two Samuel Beckett plays, though the press would have you believe I'm nothing more than a radio soap star.'

So magnetic was her charisma, so famous was Patricia Beresford's voice, that Roger LeCarre hadn't even noticed the Bishop of Exeter standing beside her in a purple cassock, a leather-bound Bible in his hand, a crucifix around his neck. Basically, he looked like your standard bishop.

'I'm afraid the Bishop is correct . . . ' Peacock announced to the room. 'It's not safe for anyone to leave here tonight. All the roads are blocked. I'm sure they'll salt them in the morning. I believe you were all intending on staying the night anyway?'

LeCarre spotted Cynthia Pest take her iPhone 13 Pro Max from her Hermès handbag and hold it to her wealthy ear.

'Yes, I was, but . . . but . . . being stuck here . . . that wasn't part of the script, and I'm an actress, I'm sure some of you may be familiar with some of my work, you can't change the script at the last minute,' said Beresford.

'You should try a day in my world,' said LeCarre. 'We don't have scripts. We have bodies. So many bodies. All we know is that when our head hits the pillow at the end of the day, *if we can find a pillow*, we're gonna close our eyes and see bodies. So many bodies.'

'Sorry, I'm just trying to work it out,' said Patricia Beresford. 'Are you a doctor?'

'Detective. Detective Roger LeCarre. Pleased to meet you, Ms Beresford. I'm an enormous fan of your work.'

Beresford responded to the compliment with a small, polite smile.

'I'm terribly sorry,' said Peacock. 'There really isn't anything we can do about the weather. As I say, I'm sure the roads will be clear in the morning. I promise we'll do our absolute best to make you comfortable while you're here. Mr Quartz is very excited to meet you all.'

'My phone!' said Cynthia Pest. 'It's dead. I can't get any reception.'

Each of the guests looked at their own device.

'Nothing,' said Little-Hope.

'Goodness gracious. Nothing at all,' said Patricia Beresford.

Despite being a satisfied customer of the largely reliable EE, even LeCarre's own Huawei P30 Pro had no service. Nothing.

'All communications are dead!' said Beresford, with typical dramatic effect.

'Not with the Lord,' said the Bishop. 'We always have a direct line to Him.'

'Of course, Your Grace,' said Beresford.

Anthony Little-Hope rolled his apparently atheist eyes.

'So just to clarify,' said LeCarre. 'None of us have ever met. We're all from completely different walks of life. We're stuck in a remote manor house. A once-in-a-generation snowstorm has cut us off from the outside world and our eccentric foreign host is yet to make an appearance?'

'That would seem to be the extent of it, yes,' said the Bishop.

'What an extraordinarily unprecedented situation,' said Beresford. 'I don't think I've ever seen the like, even in fiction. One couldn't *write* such a thing!'

# FIVE

*Crash!* The sound of a giant gong. The announcement came from the butler.

'Dinner is served! Please join your host, Mr Eli Quartz, the 23rd Earl of Devon, in the state dining room. Follow me.'

'How exciting!' said Patricia Beresford, whose mood seemed to dramatically change at the thought of seeing Eli Quartz. Or maybe it was the suggestion of food.

The party of five – Beresford, Cynthia Pest (the Duchess of Totnes), Professor Anthony Little-Hope, the Bishop of Exeter and Detective Roger LeCarre – did as they were told. Was this it? Just the five of them? It hardly seemed like the pulsating, peopled party LeCarre had been expecting. There had been more people at his last birthday dinner, for which they'd booked a table for twelve at Zizzi's on Gandy Street, although actually only eleven came because Detective Inspector Todd Gatting had texted at the last minute to say that he couldn't make it because his gout had flared up again. *Just have an avo salad and a virgin cocktail, Gatts. They really do cater for every diet*, LeCarre had texted back. No response had come and ever since LeCarre had been unsure about DI Todd Gatting. Was that the kind of guy you wanted covering your back in a firefight? A man who let a bit of gout stop him coming to your birthday dinner? LeCarre wasn't so sure.

The state dining room was darker than the music room and more medieval in tone. A huge fireplace with a selection of coats of arms above it. Wood panelling. Another golden chandelier. An enormous painting, about the size of three smaller paintings or, perhaps more helpfully, four ping-pong tables. The painting was of a family, presumably former residents, proudly posed in the weird clothes of their age. The room's centrepiece was a long, mahogany banquet table at the end of which sat the man himself – Eli Quartz, the 23rd Earl of Devon. How would that family feel if they knew that their castle would one day be owned by a tech billionaire? Confused, most likely.

Quartz stood up and held his American arms out wide.

'Welcome! All of you! Thank you so much for joining me at Powderham Castle! This is an honour.'

Quartz pronounced it 'Powder-ham' instead of the correct 'Powderum'. LeCarre winced. Americans! Why did they insist on creating their own accent? We gave them a language and we showed them how to speak it – was it really necessary for them to go so off-piste? It was like giving someone a tennis racquet and watching them try to wipe their arse with it, thought LeCarre.

His fellow guests shuffled into the room, sheepish smiles on their faces. These were all people of status in their fields, the cream of Devon. In another man's castle, a billionaire no less, they all seemed somewhat neutered. All except Detective Roger LeCarre. No man neutered Roger LeCarre. Carrie had suggested that he get a vasectomy. Fearing he may lose the source of his power, LeCarre had refused. 'We'll just do it standing up. You can't get pregnant standing up.'

The group sat down, small talk was made, wine was poured and then Quartz rose again.

'Ladies and gentlemen, I have a confession to make. I have fallen in love with your country and most especially this county. You may wonder what a little ol' sucker with nothing but a six-shooter and $76.4 billion could see in a place like Devon. Well, what isn't there to love about a place like Devon? The rolling hills, the beautiful coastline, the ancient architecture.'

He looked towards Little-Hope and the Bishop.

'The Exeter University. The cathedral. The culture . . . '

He looked at the blushing Patricia Beresford.

'I freely admit that I am new here. There is much I don't know about your county, most especially the people. All I really know are Arthur here and his daughter Angela. They've been so accommodating to their new earl. Little ol' me. I wanted so much to celebrate my purchase of Powder-ham Castle with the people of Devon. I want to be a good earl to my people. I want to be your earl. That is why I asked Arthur and Angela to put together a list of the five most important people in Devon, to come and share in my joy in becoming your county's newest Devonian. Did I say that right?! But tonight is not just a night of celebration. I've met one or two of you already, the others I'm so excited to be meeting tonight. I want to pick each and every one of your brains. There's so much I can learn from you all. I'm honoured to say that Cynthia Pest, the Duchess of Totnes, is with us this evening. Cynthia, I'd like to learn from you how to be the gracious and loved servant to your people that you are. Patricia Beresford, I'm told you have won the hearts of this county. I'd sure like to learn how you did it!'

A generous laugh from the room. Quartz was already making friends.

'Professor Anthony Little-Hope. Professor, I am a man of the future. It's how I make my money. Providing the instruments of the future. Some of which I'd like to share with you all this weekend. But, Professor, I do not forget our past and now that I am the humble custodian of this storied castle, I'd be grateful for your admired historical perspective on my new home.'

Little-Hope's flattered face grew red, syncing with his red-haired head. The guy's a nerd! thought LeCarre.

'Bishop, Your Grace, I do not pretend to be a man of God but I am a man of faith. Your presence here is very important to me.

'Last but not least, I am delighted to say that we are joined by Detective Roger LeCarre this evening. I'm told that no man has done more to keep the good people of this county safe from the disgusting scourge of crime. If nothing else, I hope your presence here tonight can leave us all confident that our wallets are safe.'

A generous titter filled the room. Quartz may have spoken with a ridiculous accent but what he did talk was sense, thought LeCarre. Eli Quartz wore a thin black turtleneck sweater with smart casual jeans. On his head was a cowboy hat and on his feet cowboy boots. LeCarre couldn't help but notice that Quartz had not kept to his own black tie dress code. Quite the power play. Was a castle not enough to denote status?

Angela and the butler that LeCarre had just learned was her father, Arthur Peacock, placed a crab, unmistakably from Devon, in front of each guest. LeCarre watched Angela move sideways along the table like the sexiest crab he'd ever seen. If only he could have her on toast.

The guests made polite conversation, occasionally interrupted by the dramatic sound of thunder. Perhaps it was God's refusal to stay quiet that led the Bishop of Exeter to move the conversation on to more controversial subject matter.

'Mr Quartz, I've read up on some of your inventions with interest,' said the Bishop.

'I'm glad to hear it, Your Grace,' said Quartz.

'I was particularly interested in your work in the field of medicine. Robot hearts.' Quartz's company had been experimenting with fitting heart patients with robot hearts. 'Very impressive. Do you ever worry that you're playing God?'

'I believe, Your Grace, that in my work in medicine, in

the work that Quartz Industries does in the field of medicine, I am, in my own very humble way, doing God's work. I could never hope to take His place. Besides, I think I'm correct in saying that there is no vacancy for the position of God. Is that right, Your Grace?'

The Bishop didn't seem satisfied with Quartz's rather odd answer but was flummoxed as to what to say.

'Yes, Mr Quartz. No vacancy,' he said.

The age-old tension between the worlds of the religious and the scientific was always there. The old versus the new.

A robot heart? What did that even mean? At least it was a heart. Carrie sometimes said she wondered if Roger had one. 'Of course I do, Carrie. That's why I'm out all night every night. Stopping crime! It's because my heart can't take it to see the suffering. I'm all heart. I'm one big heart! A heart with arms and legs that are also made of heart. Cut me open and I bleed heart, Carrie.'

Just then LeCarre's giant weird heart skipped a beat, as did the hearts of everyone else at the table. Suddenly LeCarre wondered if this was the escape from the horrors of the outside world he had hoped it might be. Because it was in that moment that he and everyone else at Powderham Castle heard a blood-curdling scream.

'Arrrgh! Arrrrgh!'

'Dear God, what's wrong?' said Anthony Little-Hope.

'There's something ... there's something under us! Arrrgh!' screamed Beresford.

And now Patricia Beresford wasn't the only screaming woman in Powderham Castle because Cynthia Pest was screaming too.

'Arrrgggh! I felt it too!' screamed Cynthia Pest.

Just then, Arthur Peacock came through purposefully holding a broom which he banged against the floor at Beresford and Pest's side of the table.

'Get out!' he shouted at the floor. 'Get out of here, go on! Get out!'

A scurrying sound went in the direction of the music room.

'I'm terribly sorry for the disturbance, ladies and gentlemen,' said Peacock. 'This is a very old castle and very old castles tend to come with the same problem ... rats.'

'Urgh!' shuddered Pest at the thought of her namesake.

'That wasn't a rat,' said Beresford. 'I felt it under my feet. It was huge!'

'They're under the floorboards, Ms Beresford,' said Peacock. 'They can bring you no harm.'

'I'm afraid it's a case of the bigger the house,' said Angela, sexily, 'the bigger the rats.'

46

She really was an angel, a sexy angel sent from above, talking about rats.

Eli Quartz leaned back in his chair.

'I said when I got here we should gas the bastards out but Mr Peacock won't let me. He's . . . you don't mind me saying so, do you, Mr Peacock? He's a little stuck in his ways. You see, the Peacocks have been here a few generations. Isn't that right, Arty?'

Arthur Peacock clenched his jaw and nodded. He didn't like being called Arty, that much was clear. Eli Quartz continued.

'Obviously, I wanna respect things the way they were, but we gotta move this place into the twenty-first century. Ain't that so, Arty? He'll see. OK . . .' Quartz clapped his hands together. 'Everybody ready for their main course?'

And with that, Quartz took a remote control from under the table. A humming sound came from the direction of the kitchen and a small procession of floating drones brought a full plate to each guest. There were howls of delight. Even LeCarre had to admit it was an impressive trick.

Quartz held up the remote control.

'I can rig this baby up to pretty much anything.'

'How wonderful!' said Patricia Beresford. 'Aren't you a clever man?'

And she was right. Quartz was a clever man but perhaps, for LeCarre's tastes, a little too keen on showing it.

'Hey, Arty!' said Quartz. 'How about we give the gang a tour after dinner?'

'Certainly, sir,' said Arthur Peacock.

# SIX

This wasn't Detective Roger LeCarre's first time in a castle. A few years ago he'd spent a full day assessing whether the National Trust or English Heritage offered the best value. In the end, he'd opted to join both and never looked back, spending many a Sunday with Carrie and Destiny, their daughter, wandering the halls of a stately home, LeCarre picking the guide up on any historical errors they were making. He took the same approach to breakdown cover, subscribing to both the AA and the RAC. There was a whole world out there and Roger LeCarre wanted to experience everything in it, and that included excessively extensive breakdown cover.

From the outside, Powderham looked like the six-hundred-year-old castle it was, sitting beside the River

Exe, overlooking an expanse of delightfully Devonian countryside. Its two Norman towers reminded visitors of its once-violent past. A time when Roundheads fought Cavaliers in a battle for the soul of Britain, much like guests on Nicky Campbell's 5 Live morning debate show did now. On the inside, it was more of a traditional English manor, although Quartz's American influence was already starting to show. Victorian rocking horses sat beside foosball tables. Marble busts of serious-looking men sat beside arcade machines.

First, he showed them the library. Eighteenth-century bookshelves stretched almost as high as the fourteen-foot-high ceilings, about the height of two basketball players. On them were hundreds of leather-bound books – although, remembering his childhood home, LeCarre wondered whether they were actually fancy plastic cases for video cassettes.

'This is the library,' said Quartz, standing in front of one of the castle's many marble fireplaces. 'Your Grace, you may be interested to know that these books contain some of the most important sermons and religious essays of the eighteenth and nineteenth centuries. Unfortunately, as you can see, they take up quite a lot of space. That is why my team at Quartz Industries will soon be transcribing them and putting them all into one ebook reader not much bigger than my hand. Isn't that amazing? That way we won't lose any of their contents, but I'll be able to burn them in this fireplace and turn the room into a man cave. Soon these walls will be covered with TVs. Isn't that great?'

'Wonderful!' said Patricia Beresford, to LeCarre's surprise. 'You're a genius, Mr Quartz!'

Ever since Eli Quartz had shown his face, Patricia Beresford had seemed to fawn over him. I guess money attracts, thought LeCarre, smartly.

'There is one feature of this room I'm very keen to keep,' said Quartz, who then made a show of pushing a bookcase and revealing a secret door.

'A secret door!' said Beresford. 'How marvellous!'

Quartz led them up a small set of stairs to a room containing a pinball machine. As their journey around the house went on, the group discovered that it was full of secret doors and passageways, so many that Quartz didn't always seem to know where they were. Anthony Little-Hope, the History professor, who'd clearly already been to Powderham Castle many times before, gradually played a larger role, aiding Quartz in his tour, chipping in with boring historical facts.

'I'm so grateful to you, Professor,' said Quartz. 'You sure do know your onions, and by onions I mean history.'

'Powderham Castle is a very special place,' said Little-Hope. 'I hope it stays that way.'

'Oh, it will, Professor, you don't need to worry about that,' said Quartz, before proudly showing them the mechanical rodeo bull he'd had installed in the nursery.

The quietest of the group was Cynthia Pest, who walked around with what appeared to be a kind of wistful sadness which will probably be elaborated on later in the book. For the others, LeCarre included, Powderham Castle was a novelty, a window into another world. Cynthia Pest was the Duchess of Totnes and, most likely, grew up in similar surroundings. Perhaps, thought LeCarre, she was pining for a long-forgotten childhood. Or perhaps the castle reminded her of a sad past, one that had led her to become the seemingly brittle woman she was today. Or maybe she was just a bit moody because she was on her period or something.

They ended back in the impressive music room in which their evening had begun, with Eli Quartz treating them to a selection of songs on the piano. It was all a bit much for Roger LeCarre, who thought he didn't mind jazz standards but would prefer people did it in the privacy of their own homes, before remembering that Eli Quartz was in his own home. Things only became unbearable when Patricia

Beresford joined Quartz to perform a number of duets from Andrew Lloyd Webber musicals.

Actors! They just didn't get the real world. Too lost in their own heads. Every couple of months LeCarre would get paired with some actor 'researching a role' who wanted to experience life as a police officer. LeCarre would punch them in the face, then again, then again.

'That's life as a police officer,' he'd say. 'Life hitting you hard. Every minute. Of every day.'

Only Brenda Blethyn hit him back. Fair play to her.

The rest of the room seemed to be enjoying Beresford and Quartz's performance. Even Arthur Peacock, the butler, couldn't help but tap his feet.

'They love us, Eli!' said Beresford. 'Maybe we should act out a scene from my radio show. Oh, what have I done with my phone? I've got the entire BBC sound effects library on there, you know. We could give it a real professional touch. No. We're in the music room. How about another song? You know, you're quite the pianist. Perhaps I should take you on tour with me.'

'Oh, I've been meaning to speak with you about that, Ms Beresford,' said Quartz.

'Yes! Yes! Let's talk!' Beresford was suddenly very excited. 'Ladies and gentlemen, I − well, we have a little announcement to make. I'm very excited to say that the Earl of Devon, my good friend Eli here, has agreed to fund my next project. This spring, after many years with *Jam on Top*, I will be leaving the show and going on a tour of England's finest theatres.'

The room was suddenly privy to information that would shake Devon to its West Country core. *Jam on Top*, the BBC Devon radio series, was Devon and Patricia Beresford was *Jam on Top*. If Devon had a stock market, it would be tumbling at the news. But Beresford's fame was incredibly localised. Step a mile into Dorset and no one knew who she was. A tour of English theatres seemed ambitious.

'My tour will be starting ... Eli, sweetie, where's my first date?'

For the first time that night, Quartz seemed uncomfortable.

'There's a few things to finalise. I'll talk to you tomorrow,' he said.

'The dates are set, though, aren't they?' said Beresford.

'Not quite,' said Quartz. 'I'm just having another look at the finances. Making sure it all adds up.'

'Making sure it all adds up? You're a billionaire!' Beresford was speaking more quietly now, but with increasing concern.

'I'm a businessman. I have to be sure it's going to be worth it for everybody.'

'Worth it?! I've already recorded my final episode of *Jam on Top*! Thelma Bertwhistle is dead!'

The room took a giant intake of breath. It was like hearing a family member had passed. Roger LeCarre knew that feeling only too well because far too many times he'd been the one who'd had to break the terrible news, and also because he'd had a pet die when he was a kid.

'Let's talk tomorrow,' said Quartz.

'Tomorrow?! No! My career depends on this. I need to know now! Is my tour happening or not?'

'I'm sorry, Patricia, I'm afraid to say ...' but Eli Quartz clearly wasn't too afraid to say because he did say, 'It isn't.'

Beresford flung a vase of flowers off the grand piano and onto the floor. LeCarre watched the water seep into the antique rug but didn't worry about it too much because water doesn't stain. The evening didn't feel much like a celebration any more. The last time LeCarre had seen a mood drop that quickly was on the night he'd told Carrie that he'd accidentally sent Destiny to school with a taser in her lunchbox. 'I'm sorry! I'm tired, I thought it was a big chocolate bar!'

Someone had to say something to break the tension.

'Perhaps the guests would like a brandy, Mr Quartz?' said Peacock.

'What an excellent idea. Yes, brandies for everyone please, Arty.'

Anthony Little-Hope sought to aid Quartz in changing the subject.

'That spear, Mr Quartz,' said Little-Hope. 'It's magnificent. Where did you get it from?'

'Oh, this,' said Quartz. 'I got it on my travels in Africa.'

'Do you mind if I take a look?' said Little-Hope.

'Not at all.'

Little-Hope held the elaborately decorated wooden spear, as tall as him, and inspected it.

'The handiwork is incredible. You must have purchased it from a tribe, yes? Which tribe? I'm afraid my knowledge of Africa is a little limited.'

'I think I got it from the gift shop at Cape Town airport,' said Quartz. 'They had so much great stuff. I bought, like, a hundred fridge magnets. Oh! Have I shown you my tusk? Ladies and gentlemen, I don't think I've shown you my tusk, have I?'

'Tusk?' said the Bishop. 'No, I don't believe you have.'

Quartz walked across the room and there the tusk was, resting on two hooks on the wall just above the fireplace.

The house was so full of enormous ornaments and antiquities that no one, at least not LeCarre, had noticed the tusk before.

'I ... I may need a little help with this. Detective? You wanna give me a hand here, buddy?' said Quartz.

LeCarre obliged and used his easily above-average strength to help Quartz take the tusk off the wall. The two men stood holding the eight-foot tusk horizontally and looking at the rest of the guests. Peacock was hanging by the door, waiting to see how the room would react. Angela, his really, really sexy daughter, had entered from the other side to see the action now taking place. She was standing by a fuse box, but LeCarre could be forgiven for thinking that all the electricity in the room came from her. LeCarre looked down at the tusk. It was ivory, the real thing, and seemed remarkably well kept for an antique.

'I got this last summer in Namibia. Isn't she a beauty?'

'What do you mean you got it in Namibia? You purchased it?' said Pest.

'No. That wouldn't be any fun. Anyone can buy a tusk. Anyone with money, anyway.'

'Mr Quartz, you don't mean to say you ... ?' said Anthony Little-Hope.

'Oh, dear God!' said Patricia Beresford.

'You bet I did! Shot the sucker myself! They see a Westerner like you or I and they charge through the roof for a hunting trip, because they know the prize is so big, but I got to tell you it was worth every goddamn cent. The feeling! It's so easy to get away from our nature, you know, to forget about what we actually are, but there I was – a real man – top of the food chain! Little ol' me conquering nature with my trusty 12-gauge!'

'You monster!' screamed Cynthia Pest, the sound so powerful that it seemed to come up from the bottom of the Earth. LeCarre had heard women scream before, usually in the throes of erotic ecstasy, not in indignant rage. LeCarre looked at a room full of people looking at Eli Quartz with pure hatred, a man who didn't seem to realise the anger he'd just provoked. Cynthia Pest's body was almost diagonal, pointed in righteous fury towards Eli Quartz. Anthony Little-Hope, who until then had been relaxing on a chair, stood up. A liberal man such as Little-Hope didn't want to be seen to luxuriate in the pleasure of an elephant hunter. The Bishop, who stood close to LeCarre, crossed himself and mumbled a prayer. By holding the tusk, LeCarre feared he might be seen as in some way complicit and was about to put his end down when the loudest sound of the night arrived in the form of a thunderbolt. It seemed to hit the castle itself.

Darkness. Sheer darkness. Blacker than the ebony keys on the piano which just ten minutes before was entertaining the room. Blacker than Eli Quartz's American Express card. Blacker than Roger LeCarre's tuxedo when he'd first bought it. Blacker than black. Black. Basically, the lights had gone out.

'Just a minute, ladies and gentlemen. Please remain calm,' said Peacock, who seemed to be scrabbling around the room in search of a solution to the sudden loss of light.

'We'll have this sorted in just a moment,' said Angela, sexily.

All LeCarre could hear was a kind of chaos. Crying, muttering, bodies stumbling around in search of light, in search of a seat. Disorientated, he felt himself bumped into and moved about. It could have been thirty seconds, it could have been five minutes, but the moment came to an end when Peacock said: 'I'm sorry, everybody. We have a backup generator. I think I've managed to find it. Let's see if this . . . '

And then the lights came on. LeCarre blinked, adjusting his eyes to the brightness. Soon it wasn't light he had to adjust to, but a new reality. A new role. A role he had cast many times before but never played himself. The role of chief suspect.

Because Patricia Beresford, Anthony Little-Hope, Cynthia Pest, Arthur and Angela Peacock, and the Bishop of Exeter were all looking at him.

LeCarre looked back at them and then at Eli Quartz who lay on the ground, dead, a huge wound to his chest.

And in Detective Roger LeCarre's hand?

A bloodied tusk.

# SEVEN

On 22 October 1975, Gerry Conlon, Paul Michael Hill, Paddy Armstrong and Carole Richardson were convicted of planting two lethal bombs in the Surrey town of Guildford a year earlier. They came to be known as the Guildford Four. In 1989, their convictions were quashed after the police were found to have tampered with evidence and to have used unlawful tactics to acquire forced confessions. To this day, it is known as one of the greatest miscarriages of justice in British legal history and was the subject of the 1994 film *In the Name of the Father*, which received seven Academy Award nominations.

Between 5 August 1962 and 11 February 1990, the South African political leader Nelson Mandela was imprisoned for his opposition to the brutal apartheid regime. In 1993, Mandela was awarded the Nobel Peace Prize and on 10

May 1994, he was inaugurated as the first Black president of South Africa and served for five years, leaving a legacy of truth, justice and forgiveness that still provides inspiration to billions around the world today.

On 6 January 2023, Detective Roger LeCarre was locked in a cupboard and told he couldn't come out until the snow had cleared and the police had arrived.

How had it come to this? LeCarre *was* the police. If you found yourself locked away in Devon and Cornwall, the chances were, Detective Roger LeCarre was the man who put you there. Not this time. The hunter had become the hunted.

This wasn't the first time Roger LeCarre had been locked up. Once, after they had had a new bathroom fitted, LeCarre had had trouble with the new lock and found himself trapped. Six hours he'd waited for Carrie to get home and let him out. Those were the most difficult six hours of his life. LeCarre was a man who didn't cope with confinement well. By the time Carrie had arrived he was just minutes from drinking bleach, simply for something to do. He'd already brushed his teeth about forty times. The only saving grace was that at least being locked in a bathroom gave him access to a toilet. Fantastic access, actually – it was right there. Not this time. This time, all he had was a bucket.

*A bucket full of thoughts.*

Two things were clear: 1) Detective Roger LeCarre was trapped in a castle with a murderer, and 2) that murderer had framed him.

The whole situation was *really annoying*.

Like the convict he now was, LeCarre took a key from his pocket and carved his name into the wall.

DETECTIVE ROGER LECARRE.

It took longer than he thought. By the time he was on the 'c' in 'Detective' he wished he'd just gone for 'Rog'. LeCarre looked around his new abode. That didn't take long. For a cupboard, it was a pretty big space. For a cell it would be in breach of every human rights convention on Earth. Most cells, these days, had enough room to swing a cat in. Not this one. Not a big cat, anyway. Maybe a kitten, and even then you wouldn't have enough room to have your arms fully outstretched.

This wasn't the life his mother had dreamed of for him. Peggy LeCarre had wanted him to become a florist. 'You'll always be surrounded by the beauty in life,' she'd said. Instead he'd spent a career surrounded by the ugly. The misery. The *crime*. Maybe he should have taken her advice, he thought, before remembering he had hay fever, so being a florist would be an absolute nightmare.

Now he was just another prisoner. Another lag. Inmate number: 0001. At least he didn't have to find out who top dog in this joint was. *He was.* LeCarre wouldn't be needing to find snouts for currency. No fears about dropping soap in the shower for him. There was no shower and there was no soap. There was just a man and his thoughts. A man who needed to get in shape and start working on his release.

LeCarre got himself face down on the ground and did a quick five hundred press-ups, then sat down on the floor, leaned back and began bouncing a small ball against the opposite wall. Don't worry about where he got the ball from. It was probably just in the cupboard already or something.

Eli Quartz. Who wanted him dead, and why? Patricia Beresford had a motive, one born out of rage. *Jam on Top* was a BBC Radio Devon institution and the character of Thelma Bertwhistle was its heart. Leaving that behind was a huge move and she'd just had the rug pulled out from under her. Quartz had giveth and Quartz had taketh away. She'd started the evening thinking the future was bright – a tour of England. Then Quartz had said there was no tour. Now her diary was empty. Leaving a popular soap opera often meant a descent into obscurity. This could have been a crime of passion, and no one was more passionate than an actress. Seriously, have you ever met one? It's a non-stop rollercoaster.

Could she have done it and, if so, how? LeCarre berated himself. He'd been right there, at the scene of the crime, inches from the murder itself, one had to presume, and yet he had no clue what had happened. The murder had to have taken place while the lights were off. That was the time frame. How long that was, he didn't know. One minute? Five? No more than that. For the first time since he'd first put on the uniform all those years ago, LeCarre had allowed himself to go 'off duty'. Chang had even sent him here on an assignment of sorts – to get to know Eli Quartz – and yet he'd recklessly switched off. Well, that assignment was over. Quartz was dead. Detective Roger LeCarre had a new assignment and that was to find his killer, but he'd have to do it from behind bars; not that he was behind bars, exactly – he was behind a cupboard door.

*Ba dum pap. Ba dum pap. Ba dum pap.*

The sound of the ball bouncing against the floor, the opposite wall and then back into LeCarre's hand. The sound of his massive mind whirring away. The wound – he'd seen it, on Quartz's bloodied chest. From his all-too-brief assessment, it seemed consistent with a tusk blow. He'd seen one before, on a zookeeper at Paignton Zoo. That was an open-and-shut case of death by rambunctious elephant. LeCarre had wanted to charge the elephant with murder. Apparently you couldn't charge animals with crime. 'Oh, so they can do what they like? The system's a joke!' LeCarre had said to his superiors, before writing to his MP and asking for a series of animal courts to be set up across the country. No response was forthcoming. This was the thing with politicians. You went to the trouble of putting together a detailed, sensible plan for an animal court system and they didn't even give you the courtesy of replying.

*This* elephant, the former owner of the tusk, hadn't had a say in the matter. There was some natural justice to it, though. The elephant Eli Quartz had killed had ultimately been used to kill him. Could the whole thing have somehow been engineered by an environmental activist? If they could glue themselves to motorways and prevent LeCarre from getting to his squash club on time – something that had happened no fewer than twice – then they were capable of anything. Cynthia Pest had appeared the most enraged. In LeCarre's experience, the animal rights activists he picked up at protests were all jobless trust fund recipients, rebelling against the parents who funded their crusty lifestyles. Crust aside, Pest certainly fit the profile.

But LeCarre had been holding the tusk the whole time.

This was what didn't make sense. All he knew was that he hadn't done it. Roger LeCarre was simply incapable of killing another human being, except on the odd occasion when he had done so, but for totally justifiable reasons.

What made LeCarre so sure the tusk had done the deed? The wound was consistent with a tusk blow, but it could have been consistent with any number of other implements. The castle was full of strange items, big and small. If he could just get out there and look at them he might be able to make some goddamn progress, but he was stuck in this goddamn cell, this cupboard.

Anthony Little-Hope had been the most insistent.

'This man is dangerous! We have to lock him away!'

Just the sort of thing he'd say if he were the actual murderer. Perhaps Devon's finest historian didn't like the rapid Americanisation of Devon's finest castle. A pity that Devon's finest copper had to take the blame.

Peacock, Little-Hope and the Bishop of Exeter had wrestled LeCarre to the ground. Sure, LeCarre had resisted his citizen's arrest but one man versus three wasn't a fair fight. Particularly two big men like Peacock and the Bishop. Both the wrong side of sixty but both with heft behind them. Had LeCarre had been in their shoes he'd have done the same but he wasn't – he was in his own iconic brown brogues (which would probably feature quite heavily in any long-running TV series that came about as a result of this series of books) and he knew he was innocent.

'The storage cupboard under the stairs!' Angela had said, sexily.

Then Little-Hope, Peacock and the Bishop had dragged him out of the music room and to the giant staircase. Pest and Beresford sat crying, heads in their hands.

'Go easy! I'm complying, goddamnit!' LeCarre had said.

Those giant turquoise walls, the stunning decorative rococo plasterwork, the Restoration oil paintings – in all their centuries, had they ever seen drama like this? Angela had opened a door under the stairs, a door you wouldn't know was there, and revealed a storage cupboard. How many other secret doorways were there in this place? Secret passageways? Secret people? Secrets? How many secrets? *HOW MANY SECRETS?!*

*Knock. Knock. Knock.*

Not the sound of the increasing madness in LeCarre's mind, but the sound of a clenched fist rapping against his cupboard door. A knock at the door, basically.

'Hello?' said a womanly voice. It was Angela, the sexy servant.

'I didn't do it!' LeCarre shouted through the door.

'Don't take us for fools, Detective. We were standing right there. We saw you do it,' said Angela.

'You didn't see me do anything. All you saw was an innocent man get framed. I take it you've called the police? I can give you their number if you like. You know, because I am them. It's ... have you got a pen? It's 9 ... 9 ... 9.'

'Very funny, Detective,' said Angela. 'All our communications are still down. I'm sure the police will be here in the morning. In the meantime, can I get you anything? Something to eat? A book?'

'You're being very kind to a murderer,' said LeCarre. 'Not that I – and I can't stress this point enough – not that I am one.'

'I happen to think that everyone deserves love, Detective,' said Angela. 'Even those who've committed crime. Sadly, that's not always the way it works.'

What kind of wishy-washy radical thinking was this? Lock them up and throw away the key! That had always been LeCarre's philosophy, although he appreciated that it wasn't necessarily a practical way of running a prison. He'd heard of a joint down in Truro where they'd tried it – throwing away all of the keys. Apparently they very quickly regretted it. Presumably just general prison maintenance necessitates the need to access the cells from time to time, and if you throw away all the keys that's not going to be possible. Also, what about when the prisoners eventually, like we all do, die? Ultimately, over time, you're going to find yourself with a load of cells with dead bodies in them and before you know it you're going to have to build a new prison. At a purely operational level, locking people up and throwing away the key is a terrible idea.

'I'm not hungry,' said LeCarre.

'Very well,' said Angela. 'I'll come and check on you in the morning.'

LeCarre listened as Angela's incredibly attractive footsteps faded away. He narrowed his eyes. Then a bit more. Then a bit more. He kept narrowing them until they were fully closed and he was asleep.

# EIGHT

*A buxom maiden, one of many, golden locks covering her pre-Industrial Revolution breasts, produced another piece of succulent meat and fed it to the handsome man who sat upon his throne in robes of many colours, a crown of jewels upon his head.*

*'How goes the morn?' said the man.*

*''Tis fair, my lord,' said his loyal servant, Pesto. 'Sun doth shine down upon this land in merry rays. Visibility is roughly fifty score metres. Which is a thousand metres, my liege.'*

*'Then we march on Cornwall this very morn, although the Tamar Bridge hasn't been built yet so we'll have to get a boat across the river.'*

*'Yes, sire. Are thou not afraid-est, my lord?'*

*'Never!' said the handsome and powerful man. 'For our fight is a righteous one. Our two counties of Devon and Cornwall must be*

*united. Only I and my army of loyal knights can achieve our des-*
*tiny. Over the horizon, I see many threats – dragons, robbers, credit*
*card fraud. This land must be protected and I, with God on my side,*
*will make it so. I will create the Devon and Cornwall police force.'*

Detective Roger LeCarre awoke. Was that a dream? Yes, obviously. Think about it. As his eyes adjusted to his surroundings he came to the realisation that sadly it had not *all* been a dream. Eli Quartz really was dead, LeCarre really had been framed for his murder, and LeCarre really was locked in the cupboard under the stairs in Devon's most famous manor house, Powderham Castle. Also, he really, really needed a piss.

It hadn't been an easy night's sleep on the floor of a cupboard in a castle, locked up for a crime he did not commit. Being underneath the stairs had made it harder. Constant footsteps throughout the night, up and down the stairs. A guilty conscience walking the castle, thinking about the murder they'd just done, the man they just framed?

*Or preparing for their next crime?*

After relieving himself into the bucket provided, LeCarre assessed the parameters of his windowless cell. A big cupboard still made for a small living space. LeCarre could hear the wind howling outside. Only then did he notice that he was shivering. How many doors were between him and the outside world? Three at least. And yet the brutal weather still found a way to reach him. It was like when Carrie was on her period. Roger could be in the bedroom upstairs, with Carrie in the downstairs toilet, but still he'd feel her frosty mood.

LeCarre took his slickly designed Huawei P30 Pro from his pocket and looked at a picture of Carrie alongside himself and their beautiful daughter Destiny. It was taken the day they took the Seaton Tramway, the East Devon tourist attraction that runs three miles along the coast from Seaton to Colyton. Roger could remember the day so well. Carrie had got Groupon tickets and persuaded Roger to join her and Destiny, but despite the overwhelmingly positive online reviews he felt that the tram was a disappointment.

'I'm sorry, Carrie, but the more I think about it, I just don't see the appeal. It only travels three miles! That's forty-five minutes, army marching pace – we might as well just walk. If trams were still worth having they'd still be everywhere. This whole day is just a reminder that public transport will lose out to the independence offered by cars. Every. Single. Time.'

That was what he loved about their relationship – they were the perfect team. She'd suggest something, he'd do it and then explain to her why it had been a bad idea. They just bounced off each other so well.

Next time he saw Carrie he could be in handcuffs. What if the murderer decided to kill him too? What if they succeeded? He had to live. He had to fight for his freedom. For their sake. Everything Detective Roger LeCarre did was for Carrie and Destiny, the women he loved. Everything except squash, which was very much his thing.

His phone still showed no sign of a signal and the battery was running down. By the sound of the weather, it could still be some time before they had any contact from the outside world. LeCarre had to clear his name and find the real killer before the police got there. If coppers arrived and found half a dozen people pointing the finger at LeCarre, that could be difficult to come back from. In his time in the force, he'd made too many enemies to be given the benefit of the doubt. LeCarre ruffled feathers: it's what he'd always done, like some kind of hands-on ornithologist. He had to start his investigation now, while he was in the castle. But he couldn't do it stuck in this damn cupboard.

The cupboard seemed to be used primarily for cleaning supplies. Mops, sprays, a broom, and a series of other items Roger LeCarre was unfamiliar with. The only cleaning he cared about was washing the streets of crime and also cleaning his Kia Ceed on a Sunday morning. If only a chamois leather could do *both* jobs with such satisfying ease.

One item caught LeCarre's eye – a robot vacuum cleaner, made by Quartz. Now that Eli Quartz was dead, would his vision of a world in which robots did all the difficult jobs be realised? Did that future end with Quartz? It couldn't, could it? Progress marches on. Or as some called it – 'Progress'. Robot cops were not something Detective Roger LeCarre was willing to contemplate. Police officers had a kind of raw human intelligence that it was impossible for science to replicate.

LeCarre stood up to stretch his legs and bumped his head on the cupboard ceiling. Crouched over but still on his feet, he noticed something for the first time. A square cut into the wood floor with a small … a small knob? Was this a trap door?

He bent down and pulled at the knob. Nothing moved. Locked? Sealed up long ago by some forgotten Earl of Devon? It had to lead somewhere, or at least it had to have once led somewhere. LeCarre was desperate for any route out of his desperate situation, wherever it led.

He pulled again, this time using some of the core leg strength that regular squash was building. Yes! It lifted up. He peered inside. Utter darkness.

It could be a basement. It could be a route out. It could be a pit of snakes. It could, for all Roger knew, be yet another branch of Pret A Manger. They seemed to be opening up everywhere. Why not here? And who could blame them? If people are willing to pay £5 for a ham sandwich then let them.

LeCarre took his Huawei P30 Pro from his pocket and activated the excellent torch function. He pointed it into the darkness. No snakes, no sandwiches. All he could see was a bottom, a couple of feet from the surface.

LeCarre swung his legs inside the cavity and rested his feet on the ground below. Standing up, he found himself waist-deep in the hole. It was at moments like these that LeCarre was thankful he hadn't let his gut expand like some of the men on the force. 'There's always a chance you might have to escape a cupboard by climbing into a really small hole,' he'd often say. He nodded to himself with the satisfaction of a man who'd been proven right.

LeCarre got down on all fours, like some kind of bovine cop, and pointed his torch ahead of him. Calling it a tunnel would be generous. This was no Eurostar and it sure as shit didn't lead to Ebbsfleet, Lille, Paris, Brussels, Rotterdam and Amsterdam and connect to cities such as Nantes and Lyon. At least he didn't *think* so. It was nothing more than a crawl space. So that's what he did – he crawled. What this was doing to the fabric of his tuxedo didn't bear thinking about.

One hand in front of the other. One knee in front of the other. His destination was not clear but anything was better than that cupboard.

Then he remembered about the rats. They'd heard them the night before. Giant rats. LeCarre bolstered himself for a possible encounter. Above ground he felt confident he could defeat a rat, however big, without much trouble. Down here? On their turf? He wasn't so sure. The space was too restrictive to allow him to unleash his full repertoire of martial arts. To beat a rat, he'd have to *become* a rat – beat them at their own game.

Just as he was slowly getting himself into the mind of a rodent, LeCarre saw a crack of light ahead. A gap in the floorboards or another trap door? This crawl space had to lead somewhere. There had to be another exit point. He sped up his crawl. LeCarre had first learned to crawl at the tender age of eight months and he hadn't done much crawling since. He was pleased to learn he still had the skill. He'd always seen crawling as a mere transitional phase on the way to learning to walk. No. He only realised it now, but it was clear. All those years ago, the baby Roger LeCarre had been training for this exact moment.

Just a few feet from the crack of light and LeCarre's world opened up. If LeCarre was travelling north to south, he now found himself at the junction of another tunnel which went east to west. In the distance on either side were more cracks of light. This was a kind of rabbit warren. Below ground there was another world of tunnels leading, LeCarre hoped, to trap doors in each room. He'd been in prison but not a high-security one. More like one of those open ones where people go for tax evasion.

It occurred to LeCarre that he had no idea of the time. It could be 3 a.m., it could be 8 a.m., it could be 5 p.m. but, on balance, that seemed highly unlikely. Five p.m. Just the thought of it made him think of ITV's hit quiz show *The Chase*. How he'd like to be sitting at home now, watching Bradley Walsh effortlessly converse with a cross-section of the British public. He had to solve this murder and get out of this damned castle. He looked at his phone: 8.27 a.m. More concerning than the time was the sight of his battery power on 4 per cent.

The original crack of light, the first one he'd seen, was closest, so LeCarre determined to continue his journey towards it. The literal light at the end of the tunnel. One hand in front of the other. One knee in front of the other. Just like when he was a baby, except in a tuxedo.

Once below it, LeCarre didn't wait – he pushed the trap door and it opened first time. What room it was, he didn't know. If the room was occupied, he might find the door slammed shut again. The other guests had all agreed to lock him away, after all. To them, Roger LeCarre was a murderer. The only thing LeCarre could murder right now was a cup of coffee but something told him no one had thought to make him one.

LeCarre didn't know what he'd find when he went through that trap door. All he knew was that he had escaped his prison cell and, like Nelson Mandela in 1990, on that beautiful day in Cape Town, he could finally, once again, call himself a free man.

# NINE

LeCarre tentatively poked his eyes above ground to find out where he was, only to discover that he was face to face with a corpse. Eli Quartz's dead American eyes looked back at him. It wasn't the first time Detective Roger LeCarre had looked at a corpse and it wouldn't be the last. LeCarre had seen more corpses than he'd had hot dinners. Sometimes he'd done both at the same time, standing in the morgue, inspecting cadavers while chowing down on a plate of chicken tikka masala fresh from the microwave. This was what he did. He looked intently into the eyes of dead bodies and then he solved their murders.

He pulled himself up and stood in the music room. LeCarre was alone. Well, not quite alone. Eli Quartz was with him, but he didn't appear to have moved since his inexplicable murder the night before.

Morning light shone through from the rose garden. Beyond that was the River Exe that led to Exeter. Just eight miles away but it felt like a million, or at least a lot more than eight. A glare came not just from the sun but the snow as well. So much snow. More than LeCarre had ever seen in person. Devon had always been a cold, cold place, he felt. More hate than love, more crime than order. A frozen wasteland of feral wolves out for themselves. It was like the weather was finally catching up with the county as it was. Devon was a tundra, devoid of morality. Detective Roger LeCarre saw himself as a giant fur, wrapping himself around the citizens and protecting them from the cold, which in this metaphor stands for crime.

From where LeCarre stood, its beauty was plain to see. Devon was still worth fighting for. Even if its earl was dead. Its earl was dead! Did this leave them vulnerable to attack from neighbouring counties? LeCarre wouldn't allow it. No. He'd bring the killer to justice and then he'd clean up the county, inch by inch, villain by villain. Once the snow had cleared, obviously. Trying to do anything outdoors right now would be an absolute nightmare.

LeCarre and Quartz, the cop and the corpse, alone together in the music room at Powderham Castle. This was *their* time. LeCarre had to use this time well, before he was discovered. This was his chance to gather the vital evidence that would solve the case and clear his name.

Quartz was flat on his back, his chest wound still gaping. Whatever hit him, elephant tusk or otherwise, appeared to have broken through his ribcage and pierced his heart. To your average citizen, such a sight might provoke a stomach churn. The only thing churning in that room was Detective Roger LeCarre's massive mind.

From what he could see, there was only one entry point. So, one blow. One almighty blow sending Eli Quartz back and onto the ground where he now lay. Quartz's hands were by his sides. He didn't look as if he'd got his arms out to break his fall. Get a blow like that and you don't have time to do anything.

So he fell straight back? Then he must have taken a hit to the back of his head as he fell. LeCarre crouched down to take a look. Nothing. Interesting. No time for a proper post-mortem, not now. LeCarre's favourite forensic Gita Patel wasn't invited to the party, unfortunately. (In fact, thinking about it, the guest list was incredibly non-diverse and if this were to go to TV, the ethnicity of some of the characters could potentially be changed to satisfy any quotas the broadcaster may have.) At first glance, the only sign of injury anywhere on Quartz's body was the blow to the chest. That's not to say that there couldn't be some bruising under his clothes. LeCarre had no intention of looking. Still being the chief suspect, the last thing he needed was for someone to walk in on him stripping the corpse. He'd been caught in a similar misunderstanding once before and had only recently been cleared of any wrongdoing by the inquiry.

The tusk. It was still on the ground, where LeCarre had dropped it in shock the night before. Still bloodied at the tip. Could someone else have used the tusk to kill Quartz while it was in LeCarre's hands? He was disorientated, he'd had a few drinks, the lights were out, but surely he'd have felt that? He remembered being bumped around in the darkness a little. Enough that the object he was holding was able to kill a man without him knowing? It didn't seem likely. Detective Roger LeCarre wasn't an easy man to shift. He had, for example, stubbornly insisted that the internet would never take off well into the noughties.

Back to the wound. He leaned in and looked at it intently. Through Quartz's turtleneck, through his chest and into his heart. What a way to go!

*His chest.*

LeCarre hadn't killed Eli Quartz but he tried to imagine for a moment that he had. He'd stood there holding the tusk horizontally, arms wrapped around it. The tusk was level with his own gut. The tusk was heavy. That's not to say that LeCarre couldn't have raised the tusk above his own head, but why would he? Quartz was not a short man. About the same height as LeCarre, he thought. When LeCarre was holding it, the night before, the tusk had been aimed directly at Quartz's gut. So if LeCarre had wanted to kill him, in the darkness, wouldn't he have jabbed the tusk into his gut? Quite apart from the madness of committing such a crime in front of everyone, unusual murder weapon in hand. That didn't mean he hadn't done it. People did crazy things all the time. Have you seen some of the hairstyles out there these days? I mean ... come on! What truly didn't make sense, for anyone wanting to prosecute LeCarre, was that 'LeCarre the murderer' hadn't chosen to jab the tusk into Quartz's gut and yet the tusk had been poised in the perfect position to do just that.

Furthermore, as far as LeCarre could see, the wound indicated a downward stabbing motion. So whoever inflicted it had most likely held the weapon above their own head and viciously jutted it down into Quartz's chest.

LeCarre got down on the ground and lay beside Eli Quartz. Two men – one dead, one alive. Both the best in their fields. Quartz and LeCarre were the same height, about the same age. Had you switched their upbringings, would you have switched their outcomes? Had Roger LeCarre not grown up on the mean streets of Totnes, born to a dentist father and a part-time ceramic artist mother, might he have become an American tech billionaire? He had the brains, he had the drive and, thanks to having watched a few episodes of *The Gadget Show* on Channel 5, he had the knowhow.

No. This is what he was. A detective. The finest detective the West Country had ever seen, and lying down beside Eli Quartz right now, he realised he could prove that he was not the man who'd murdered him. The trick now was to find the person who had.

# TEN

Detective Roger LeCarre could hear the murmur of people eating breakfast coming from the state dining room. Time to make himself known. He had already metamorphosed into his natural form – a copper, working a case. To them, he would be an escaped murderer. He had to do some explaining and he had to do it quick, otherwise he'd be back in the cupboard.

*No one wanted to be in the cupboard.*

LeCarre bounded through the library and into the dining room. The guests, all of them, were seated at the long banquet table, eating toast with marmalade, a roaring fire keeping them warm. 'Good morning!' he declared, as if it were true.

'Argh! Argh!' screamed Patricia Beresford, Devon's most famous radio actress.

'He's here! The detective! He's here!' screamed Cynthia Pest, the Duchess of Totnes.

'How did you ...?' spluttered Peacock, the butler, who stood by the far door, looking for some kind of implement to defend himself with.

'How do you think? Let me teach you the first rule of running a prison, Peacock,' said LeCarre. 'Don't have trap doors in your cells.'

'He found it!' Peacock cursed himself.

'There was a way out?' said Professor Anthony Little-Hope, the red-haired Exeter University academic. 'We have to deal with this now! The man is dangerous.'

'Don't worry, Professor,' said Peacock. 'You're outnumbered, LeCarre. There are plenty of places in this castle we can lock you away. And that's what we're going to do until the police get here.'

'*I AM THE POLICE!*' LeCarre spoke with an authority that demanded to be listened to. He'd learned from Channel 4's Supernanny, Jo Frost, to use a firm tone of voice when you need to be heard. 'Look, I didn't kill Eli Quartz but I know why you think I did. Because you're a bunch of amateurs, that's why. A bunch of amateurs! You see a dead guy on the ground and a man opposite him holding a bloodied elephant tusk and you think to yourselves, "He's the murderer! Case closed!" Well, let me tell you – case *not* closed. Case not closed at all.'

'This is nonsense,' said Patricia Beresford. 'Get him in the cupboard!'

'I think we should at least hear the man out,' said Little-Hope.

'Really? Nothing he can say can explain away what I saw with my own eyes,' said Pest.

'Look, I can go back in the cupboard, or wherever else you want to put me in this godforsaken place, but what if I'm telling the truth? If I didn't kill Quartz then that means that somebody else did. Maybe one of you. If that's the case, do the innocent amongst you want the best copper this side of Swindon working the case, or do you want him locked in a cupboard while you have tea and toast with a murderer?'

'You say you can prove you didn't do it. How?' said Little-Hope.

'I suppose we could listen for a moment,' said Peacock, picking up a brass poker from the fireplace. 'But make a move and you'll regret it.'

'Understood,' said LeCarre, calmly sitting down at the table like some kind of cool character in a film. 'Angela? Would you mind passing the butter?'

Angela, the extraordinarily sexy servant, did as he asked, her eyes never moving from LeCarre.

'Mmm, Lurpak. Denmark's finest. How could I expect anything else? We are in Devon's grandest manor house, after all. Look at us, living the good life, and yet crime still found us here, in a fortified castle. Maybe you, the elite, will take a moment to think about those of us who face down crime every day. Lurpak! I should be so lucky. Peacock, I just have to warn you – I'm about to pick up a knife.'

Peacock nodded. LeCarre spread butter on his toast. Then marmalade. He took a bite.

'Toast is cold,' said LeCarre. 'Serves me right for arriving late for breakfast. You see, I was in the music room, taking a look at a cadaver. Eli Quartz's cadaver. You all know how he died, at least you all *think* you do. A stab to the chest, courtesy of the elephant tusk I was holding. Am I right?'

The room nodded in unison.

'You're half correct. Somebody did stab Eli Quartz, but it wasn't me. I might seem tough on the outside, but the truth is I couldn't stab a fly. Whoever stabbed Eli Quartz did so like this ... '

LeCarre lifted his butter knife with two hands, above his head. Patricia Beresford gasped her familiar gasp. The one they'd all heard her do as Thelma Bertwhistle a million times before.

'They jutted the murder weapon down into Quartz's chest,' said LeCarre, 'creating the wound that killed him. I hope that rug is insured, Mr Peacock. I'm afraid to say there's rather a lot of blood on it and blood, well, blood is hard to budge.'

'I don't understand,' said Cynthia Pest. 'How does that explain that you didn't do it? We all saw you holding the tusk, we all saw the blood.'

'My dear Duchess,' said LeCarre, a little weirdly. 'I don't know exactly how many murders I've investigated but this isn't my first rodeo, by which I mean this isn't the first murder I've investigated. Far from it. Once we know the height of the wound and the trajectory of the blow we can determine the height of the attacker. *That's science.* Luckily, I carry a tape measure with me everywhere. I've already made my calculations and I can tell you all now, with absolute certainty, that whoever killed Eli Quartz was five feet five inches . . . no, hang on, I've got it written down here, was five feet eight inches tall. And I, ladies and gentlemen, am five foot ten. The fact is that I didn't murder Eli Quartz because it was simply biologically impossible for me to have done so.'

The room seemed to pause, while each of its occupants considered LeCarre's words.

'It makes sense,' said Little-Hope.

'I have to concede that it does,' said the Bishop of Exeter.

'Extraordinary. As extraordinary as one of the many storylines my beloved character, Thelma Bertwhistle, has been involved with in the BBC Radio Devon soap opera *Jam on Top*,' said Patricia Beresford, leaning back in admiration.

'You're a very clever man,' said Arthur Peacock.

'You don't win the Crown and Goose pub quiz five weeks in a row without knowing a thing or two. Is there any tea left?' said LeCarre.

Angela walked over and poured him some, sexily.

'So that's it!' said Pest. 'We're just going to believe he's innocent, the man we all saw standing there with the murder weapon, just because he threw some numbers at us?'

'I'm as perplexed as you,' said the Bishop. 'But it would seem there's nothing we can say. This man clearly did not kill Eli Quartz and that's the end of it.'

'He's right,' said Peacock. 'Detective LeCarre, I'd like to offer you my sincerest apologies. Being locked away for a crime you did not commit. What a terrible, terrible thing. I'm sorry.'

'That's quite all right, Peacock,' said LeCarre, taking his tape measure from his pocket. 'Now if I could ask everybody to stand up. I have some measuring to do.'

# ELEVEN

The results were astounding. No one could quite believe it. From the second they all stood up it was clear that there could be a problem.

Detective Roger LeCarre was supposed to be doing what detectives did – eliminating suspects, homing in on the murderer, dragging them one step closer to HMP Exeter. If one of them, and only one of them, was five feet eight inches tall, then that would be that – they'd have their man. Or woman. Women could murder too. LeCarre had seen it all too many times. Women could do anything men could do (except juggle), and that included murder. Just last month he'd charged a woman for murdering a friend with a stiletto heel. Women were dangerous, but LeCarre lived for danger. Danger, his family and squash.

Each suspect – Cynthia Pest, Patricia Beresford, Anthony

Little-Hope, the Bishop of Exeter, Arthur and Angela Peacock – stood in a line. LeCarre looked at them in astonishment. If he had a ten-foot-long spirit level and placed it on their heads he'd have a perfectly centred bubble. They were the same height. All of them.

'This is ridiculous!' said Pest.

LeCarre stepped up to Angela Peacock, bathing himself in her powerful sensual aura. He extended his tape measure, not euphemistically but literally. 'I think it's a little easier if I do it from behind,' he said, moving around her luxurious body, like a sculptor admiring his work.

LeCarre placed the lip of the tape measure under his foot and slowly moved it up to the top of her head, taking in every inch of her, but not in a sexual way, just because that was literally what he was meant to be doing.

'Incredible,' he said.

'What is it?' said the Bishop of Exeter.

'Five feet eight inches. She's five feet eight inches. *You're all five feet eight inches.*'

'I can't take this!' said Cynthia Pest, walking towards the door by the castle's entryway, hands holding her neurotic royal head. 'I have to get out of here!'

'You stay right there, goddammit,' said LeCarre, using his Supernanny voice. 'Nobody goes anywhere until I say so.'

Cynthia Pest was showing signs of withdrawal. From cocaine, no doubt. Meanwhile, Roger LeCarre was in the midst of an overdose of something else – drama.

'We can't go anywhere, anyway,' said Anthony Little-Hope. 'The snowstorm hasn't lifted; we're still cut off.'

'Oh heavens, really? I'm supposed to be meeting a friend at Café Rouge for lunch at 12 o'clock. What a ghastly situation,' said Patricia Beresford.

'I'm afraid, Ms Beresford, your glamorous lifestyle is on hold and it may be for quite some time if you prove to be the murderer,' said LeCarre.

'How dare you?' said Beresford.

'Is it really necessary to be throwing around accusations?' said the Bishop. 'Ms Beresford is this county's finest radio actress. I think she deserves some respect.'

'Throwing around accusations is my job, Your Grace. I throw around accusations like you throw around Bibles. If that is what you do. I'm sorry, I haven't been to church in a while.'

'She has a motive,' said Little-Hope.

'I do beg your pardon!' said Beresford.

'That's right, she does,' said Peacock.

'What on earth are you talking about?' said Beresford, her face blushing as red as Little-Hope's head.

'Last night,' said Little-Hope, 'Eli Quartz told you that your tour was cancelled. You seemed awfully angry.'

'Oh my God! I don't think I've ever seen someone so angry!' said Pest. 'She did it! She killed Walter Kernow and she killed Eli Quartz!'

'My dear, you are mixing up fiction with fact,' said Beresford.

Walter Kernow's killing had been *Jam on Top*'s most outrageous storyline. The episode in which Thelma Bertwhistle was convicted of his murder had stopped Devon in its tracks and was the highest-rated radio show in the county's history. Children were given the day off school to listen to it, construction sites ceased work. Even at LeCarre's own workplace, Central Exeter Police Station, everything came to a standstill. Coppers sat with criminals, good sat with evil and listened in unison, mouths gaping, as Thelma Bertwhistle met her fate.

'Now, now, I don't think Ms Beresford should be persecuted for her acting career, that doesn't seem fair,' said Little-Hope. 'I'm sure Detective LeCarre will carry out a fair-minded investigation. How will you be going about your work, Detective? I'd be happy to assist you in any way I can.'

'How's the weather situation, Peacock? How much longer are we likely to be cut off?' asked LeCarre.

'All communications are still down, sir, and the road out must be ten feet deep by now. I'm afraid we're in for another night.'

'Can't we order a helicopter or something?' said Pest.

'And how do you propose we do that, Ms Pest?' said LeCarre. 'With a giant bat signal? A big light but with a picture of a helicopter on it? No. I'd like to interview each of you today, as part of my investigation. In the meantime, you should all be very careful. There could be a murderer amongst you, after all.'

LeCarre liked the challenge element the weekend was presenting him with. Solve the murder before the snow clears. Wouldn't that be nice? Call up Chang and get her over to the castle – there's been a murder and here's the murderer for you, all wrapped up with a little bow. Another arrest for his tally.

'Detective?' said Anthony Little-Hope.

'Yes, Professor?'

'I notice you said that the murderer *could* be amongst us. Surely, we know that the murderer is amongst us. There's nobody else here. We were the only people in the room when Mr Quartz died.'

'You're forgetting one other possibility,' said LeCarre.

'Not ... not suicide?' said Beresford.

'With an elephant tusk?' said Pest, in regal incredulity.

'No. Not suicide,' said LeCarre. 'The castle became cut off sometime early yesterday evening. But we were all able to arrive before 7 p.m. Who's to say that we, the people in this room, are the only people who did so? Who's to say we're alone in this castle?'

'My God!' said Little-Hope.

The Bishop of Exeter crossed himself.

'How many rooms does this castle have, Mr Peacock?' asked LeCarre.

'I'm not sure of the exact number, Detective,' said Peacock.

'There you go,' said LeCarre. 'Too many to count.'

LeCarre made a mental note to check the property's value on Zoopla when he got back home. A three-bedroomed semi cost an arm and a leg. This place must be worth a whole body.

He continued, 'A murderer could easily be hiding somewhere in this castle. We're cut off. That works both to our advantage and our disadvantage. It means the murderer was unable to escape. That means we have a chance of catching them before the snow clears. What it also means is—'

'They may catch us first,' said Peacock.

'That's right, Peacock,' said LeCarre. 'I suggest we search the house. We can't go as one large group. We need to cover as much ground as possible, as quickly as possible, so we'll pair up. Ms Pest, you go with Professor Little-Hope. You can cover the upstairs. Mr Peacock, Miss Peacock, you can search this part of the house, the library, the music room, any alcoves or hidden rooms. I assume you both know it very well?'

'Of course, Detective,' said Angela Peacock.

'Your Grace, you and I will search the servants' quarters, the kitchen, the servants' bedrooms. I know it's your territory, Mr Peacock, but I think that means it's best somebody else searches that area. Do you understand?'

'Of course, Detective,' said Peacock.

'And what of me?' said Patricia Beresford, clearly unused to not being the centre of attention. 'Am I to simply curl up into a little ball and die?'

'Of course not,' said LeCarre. 'Somebody needs to stay here. To hold the fort, so to speak. Ms Beresford, would you be comfortable doing that? See it as an opportunity to take the weight off your feet and sit down for a while.'

'Detective! I know I'm the oldest person here, but I'm not ready for the glue factory just yet. I'll have you know my agent says my playing age is still thirty-five to forty-five!'

LeCarre realised he'd have to massage her theatrical ego.

'Ms Beresford, I presume you have experience with improvisation?'

'Experience?' said Beresford. 'I invented improvisation!'

'Good,' said LeCarre. 'Then if you do face the killer alone, while sitting here, you'll be the most able to use your skills to delay them until the rest of us return.'

Beresford inhaled with pride.

'Yes,' she said. 'Yes, I can see how that makes sense. I can do that for you.'

'Good,' said LeCarre. 'Thank you, Ms Beresford. Now, let's all go about our work. Do it quickly but do it thoroughly, and for God's sake come back alive.'

# TWELVE

The servants' quarters were down some side-stairs, below ground and away from the rest of the house. The working classes, LeCarre figured, were best off hidden away. At least that's the way the many earls of Devon would have seen it.

LeCarre had always transcended class. You couldn't put him in a box. Except on that one occasion when he and Detective LeBron Jax were searching a warehouse and Jax quite literally put LeCarre in a giant cardboard box as a joke. Good times.

LeCarre didn't care what class you came from, as long as you obeyed the law. No one was above the law. Not even God. Although the practicalities of arresting a deity didn't bear thinking about.

First, they came to the servants' dining room and kitchen.

A long table, not dissimilar to the one in the state dining room in size, but certainly in quality. This was shoddy, unvarnished wood, not the refined mahogany they'd sat at at breakfast.

LeCarre started frantically opening doors of cupboards and appliances. The killer could be anywhere – although, if LeCarre was honest with himself, unless they were some kind of otherworldly shape-shifting creature, the top shelf of the dishwasher seemed unlikely.

'It doesn't seem right, does it?' said the Bishop.

'What's that?' said LeCarre.

'That one man should have so much, and others so little.'

Here we go, thought LeCarre. Brace yourself. He could spot a socialist sermon coming from a mile off.

'Such wealth!' said the Bishop. 'And yet the people who served him live such humble lives. He had more than any man could ever need. Had he shared his worth, so many more could have lived in the kind of comfort he enjoyed.'

LeCarre had heard it all before. Sharing sounds great in theory. It's in practice that it all falls apart. It happened at the Crown and Goose all the time. Someone would buy a bag of crisps, open them and place them in the centre of the table. Great. *Mi crispa, su crispa.* What ended up happening was that one man, usually DI Todd Gatting, would eat quicker than the others and end up with more crisps. Others would take one, lick their fingers, then put their dirty hand in for more. When LeCarre got round to the bag, there'd be nothing but crumbs left, the crumbs of a flavour LeCarre would have never chosen for himself. People always said you couldn't dismiss Marxism because it had never been properly tried. Well, they tried it at the Crown and Goose and LeCarre was sorry to report that it didn't work. Better that each man saved up and bought his own bag of crisps, thought LeCarre.

'Do you know, he asked me last night if he could buy Exeter Cathedral?' said the Bishop. '*He wanted to buy Exeter Cathedral!* Told me he wanted to install an ice rink. The man had no respect for Devon. No respect at all.'

'Well, he's dead now,' said LeCarre. 'No need for you to get your ice skates on just yet, Your Grace.'

The Bishop didn't laugh. Just stared ahead in pious rage.

'It looks like there's more rooms this way,' said LeCarre and the Bishop followed.

The bedrooms of Arthur and Angela Peacock revealed little. Certainly not a hiding murderer. Arthur's room was plain, simple. A neatly made bed, a television, some Lee Child books on his bedside table. Angela's hinted at an interest in the world beyond Powderham. On her wall was a map of the world. PUT A PIN IN THE PLACES YOU'VE VISITED, said the banner at the top. On her dressing table was a box of drawing pins. Only one had made its way onto the map – Devon. There was one more bedroom, a spare room from the looks of it. No killer to be found. Just a bed with no sheets, some Wrigley's Extra Spearmint wrappers on a bedside table.

'We should get back, I suppose,' said the Bishop.

LeCarre nodded.

They climbed the stairs, back towards the state dining room, but then LeCarre stopped and gestured for the Bishop of Exeter to do the same. Someone was talking. Patricia Beresford.

'Well, you better get here quick,' Beresford could be heard to say. 'Please don't do this to me. I'm tired of living a lie. I love you.'

Love who? Who was she talking to? Not on the phone, surely? All communications were down. The Bishop cleared his throat and Patricia let out a muffled murmur of surprise. Their cover blown, LeCarre and the Bishop entered the state dining room. They were the first to return. Beresford was still alone.

Gradually, the others returned. No one had found anyone. Not Pest and Little-Hope upstairs. Not the Peacocks in the rest of the house.

Little-Hope was the first to ask the obvious question.

'Does this mean . . . ?'

'Yes,' said LeCarre, sitting down to deliver the truth. 'Yes, I'm afraid it does. The killer is amongst us.'

There was a brief pause while everyone contemplated the situation. They stared at each other, one by one. Eyes narrowing, eyes widening, eyes doing all kinds of things.

'Detective LeCarre?' said the Bishop.

'Yes?' said LeCarre.

'There is the small matter of the body.'

The body. LeCarre had forgotten for a moment about the body. Quartz was still on the floor of the music room.

'It feels rather disrespectful to leave it as it is,' said the Bishop.

Disrespectful? The Bishop hadn't had much respect for Quartz just moments before, when alone with LeCarre. Keeping up appearances for the group?

'I'm not sure we should be worrying about that,' said Pest. 'The man doesn't deserve respect.'

Every eye in the room, twelve in total, whipped in the direction of Pest.

'What?!' said Pest. 'I didn't kill him, but the man was ghastly. We all thought it.'

'He was one of God's children,' said the Bishop, religiously.

'He was an elephant-murdering bastard,' said Pest. 'The

man wasn't even the real Earl of Devon. He just purchased the title like one might walk into a shop and purchase a . . . a . . . '

'A KitKat Chunky?' said LeCarre.

'Yes! A KitKat Chunky!' said Pest.

'That may be, but the man deserves some kind of ceremony,' said the Bishop.

'Isn't there a chapel here at the castle?' said Little-Hope.

'There is,' said Peacock.

'Yes, it's just beside the rose garden,' said Angela, sexily. 'We just searched it. Empty.'

'Would you like to conduct some kind of funeral, Your Grace? I suppose it does seem rather appropriate,' said Beresford.

'Yes, if everybody is amenable to that, yes,' said the Bishop.

'There is something we do need to address, if you don't mind me saying so.' Peacock, despite the circumstances, was still maintaining his role as a loyal upright butler and hospitable host.

'Yes?' said the Bishop.

'One of us, I'm pointing no fingers, but one of us is a murderer, which means the rest of us here are at risk. Detective, I wonder, is there anything you think we should be doing to keep ourselves safe?' said Peacock.

'OK, put your hand up if you know capoeira?' said

LeCarre. 'No? Karate? Mixed martial arts? Ju-jutsu? Seriously, no one knows ju-jutsu? Jeeeeeeesus Christ. OK, here's what we're going to do. Peacock – Quartz, he had a gun, yes? Is it here at the castle?'

'Yes, it's in his gun cabinet,' said Peacock.

'Just the one gun?' said LeCarre.

'Yes. Just the one. His 12-gauge. The one he killed the elephant with, I think,' said Peacock. Pest shuddered.

'Good,' said LeCarre. 'Right. In a moment, Peacock, you're going to hand me the key to the cabinet and you're going to take me to the gun.'

Peacock nodded.

'And to the killer, let me say this.'

LeCarre swivelled his Georgian chair around and sat on it with its back touching his torso, giving him the look of a dynamic teacher telling home truths in an inner-city school.

'I'm a fair man. Anyone who's played snooker with me knows that. If I accidentally touch a ball, I let you know. I want you to meet justice courtesy of Her Majesty's Prison Service. But if you come close to threatening the safety of anyone else this weekend, I will not flinch, I will not hesitate, I will pump you full of lead – which, by the way, is what bullets are made out of. Let me clarify. Because I don't want there to be any misunderstandings. I hate misunderstandings. It's why I don't like Shakespeare. You never have a clue what they're on about. I like things to be clear, short and to the point. What I'm saying is – if you, this is the murderer I'm talking to now, who, as we've already established is one of you, one of the people I'm talking to now, but we don't know who – if you, the murderer, the person who killed Eli Quartz, the American tech billionaire who purchased this castle and the title of Earl of Devon, if you try to hurt anyone, I will shoot you. With a gun. Everyone clear? Good. OK, let's go have a funeral.'

# THIRTEEN

Detective Roger LeCarre hated funerals. He'd been to far too many. It wasn't the uncomfortable seating that bothered him. It wasn't the boring poems. It wasn't even the consistently low standard of sandwiches provided afterwards. No. It was the death. Even if you loved funerals, even if they were your favourite thing to do, you had to admit that for a funeral to happen, someone had to die. That was the way it was and unless someone changed the rules, that was the way it always would be.

Why did God have to let people die? It was a childish question with a very grown-up answer. Because God understands that if everyone lived for eternity, the strain on the pension system would become unmanageable. It would be bankrupt within ten years. *That's* why God had to let people die. LeCarre understood that, but it didn't make it any easier. So much death. So much pain. He felt like some kind of grim reaper. If you saw LeCarre, death was near. Except LeCarre wasn't there to collect your soul, he was there to collect your evidence. Every last scrap.

Powderham Castle's chapel was a small church, big enough to seat fifty people, extending from the music room and into the rose garden. LeCarre had always wanted to build an extension, although his would have a snooker table rather than a place of worship. Each to his own. Some derived meaning from ancient texts translated from ancient languages, claiming to be the word of God. Others could derive it from an accurately struck mid-range pot.

Eli Quartz lay dead on the altar: an open-casket funeral without a casket. Considering the event was conceived as a means of showing respect for the dead, Quartz's journey to the chapel had been an undignified one. Peacock, Little-Hope, the Bishop and Patricia Beresford had dragged him there, his head bumping against furniture as they went, LeCarre holding his newly acquired gun and shouting instructions.

It wasn't often that LeCarre got to hold a gun. Quartz's 12-gauge shotgun sat on his lap. He stroked it like it was some kind of lethal, metal cat. LeCarre had often wondered why British cops weren't allowed guns. American cops were and that didn't seem to cause any problems. It was another case of Britain's ridiculous health and safety culture spoiling everything. Kids weren't allowed to play conkers any more and you had to wash your hands after you used the toilet and you weren't allowed to bring a gun to work. 'You can't wrap everyone in cotton wool!' LeCarre would say, every time he reluctantly put on a seatbelt.

LeCarre's mind turned to the dead man. No friends or family. Did Quartz have any? He'd run across an ocean to settle in Devon and yet, it would appear, he had no connections or roots here. Was he running away from something? Whatever the truth, death had found him, right here on the banks of the River Exe.

LeCarre wasn't religious, not in a formal sense, but he could appreciate the simple beauty of the chapel. For LeCarre, God was an energy, floating from place to place, bouncing off people, ricocheting off walls, like a squash ball. LeCarre didn't need a Bible to tell him what God was. God was with him wherever he went. He could hear him. *Boing! Boing! Boing! That was God. Boing! Boing!*

He looked at the Bishop of Exeter, standing behind the corpse-strewn altar in his purple cassock, reading from his Book of Common Prayer. The words washed over LeCarre, his crime-occupied brain unable to catch one and comprehend it. The Bishop's deep and pious voice did not demand to be heard. Only the burning questions rang around LeCarre's mind – who killed Eli Quartz, how did they do it, and why did they frame Detective Roger LeCarre?

He had to believe that the entire congregation was capable. Even the sweetest old ladies could do the wickedest things. One case had always stayed with LeCarre. A ninety-four-year-old woman from Tiverton. Went to church on Sundays, volunteered at a homeless shelter, saved up to buy the neighbours' kids gifts at Christmas and yet she – even she, this sweet old lady – went a full three months without paying her TV licence.

'I didn't know! My son! He always sorts out things like that but he's in hospital!'

'Save it for the judge!' LeCarre had said as he hurled her into the back of a police van, like a child throwing bread for ducks.

LeCarre had learned a lesson that day. Crime could come from the unlikeliest of sources. If that old lady could do *that*, then any one of the people at Powderham Castle could have killed Eli Quartz. Even the Bishop of Exeter.

'How shall we remember him? This child of God, this Eli Quartz. Shall we remember him for the man we met last night? The brash American? The man who put money, power, status, over faith? Do you know, he asked me if he could buy Exeter Cathedral? He wanted to *buy* Exeter Cathedral!'

Quartz's interest in purchasing the cathedral had really offended the Bishop. As eulogies go, it wasn't the most complimentary LeCarre had ever heard. He'd appeared upset by the thought of robot hearts the night before as well.

'We must not judge Eli Quartz for the life he led. Some of us here, we knew the last Earl of Devon. A humble man, who loved his county. Some of us, we may have looked at Eli Quartz and wondered how such a man could be possessed of such audacity to think that *he* could take our last earl's place. Fool's pride, we might say. But Eli Quartz was a man who thought he could challenge the Creator and become, himself, a god of sorts. That may well have been his undoing. Judgement is not ours to make. Death need not be an end but a beginning. Here on Earth, in the living world, Eli Quartz was an affront to God. In the next life, he can be His servant. We must thank the Lord for His mercy in providing such a blessed opportunity. And now, let us pray ... '

LeCarre had never heard such disdain for the dead. Could the Bishop have killed Quartz, in a fit of religious zeal? Were Quartz's inventions really an affront to God? Can science go too far? Where does it end? You start with Tamagotchis, digital watches, Sky Planners. Then you move on to robot hearts, and before long the world is an army of androids, with no need for God's children. LeCarre was no Luddite. He'd allowed technology to creep into every corner of his life. He started every day with the words, 'Alexa! Make my breakfast!' But LeCarre could see how for the Bishop of Exeter, a man of God, Eli Quartz's presence in his county was an offence.

LeCarre looked into the Bishop's dark eyes, his black, black pupils, surrounded by brown and then white at the edges. Pretty normal eyes, to be fair. LeCarre looked at them and wondered if he was looking into the eyes of a killer. Not a lamb of God but a soldier of God, a kind of preaching terminator, meting out justice on His behalf, collecting sinners and delivering them to Him for redemption in the other world.

It seemed the Bishop knew the castle. He'd been there many times, no doubt. Probably knew it better than Quartz himself. Certainly better than LeCarre. That knowledge could perhaps have enabled him, somehow, to engineer

Quartz's death and place Detective Roger LeCarre in the role of murderer.

Why frame LeCarre? Collateral damage. Someone had to take the blame. Why not the police officer? God was the ultimate judge. Police were just petty underlings in the living realm. The Bishop of Exeter had to be free to continue God's work. When you are working for God, the life of one man is but a grain of sand, a speck of dust, a crumb of KitKat Chunky. Mmmm, KitKat Chunky. LeCarre hadn't had one in at least twenty-four hours. He had to get out of here and taste that perfect milk chocolate and wafer combination again. Out of this castle and back into the bright lights of Exeter. A manor house, surrounded by livestock on rolling hills. This was not his world. *His* world was the urban jungle of Exeter city centre, a world where culture and crime sat side by side, a world he understood, a world where he was King of the Jungle and you were never more than two hundred yards from somewhere you could purchase a KitKat Chunky.

Just an hour before, LeCarre had been chief suspect. Now, in his mind, he'd passed that burden on to the Bishop. Tag! He stared at him as if there were a tractor beam of light between the two men. If you did this, thought LeCarre, I will make sure that you meet justice in *this* world, not the next. Courtesy of Exeter Crown Court, although there's a bit of a backlog there so I can see the trial getting moved to Plymouth.

But they were all still suspects. *All of them.* In the front pew was Patricia Beresford, kneeling on the ground, her hands in prayer. Praying for forgiveness? Beside LeCarre was Anthony Little-Hope, deep in thought. Thinking of the murder he committed or thinking professor thoughts like, What's the square root of seventy-six? In the back pew was Cynthia Pest, her feet up in disdain. The thirty-something surly teenager of the group with no desire to hide her hatred for the victim. Standing by the door were the Peacocks, Arthur and his beautiful daughter, Angela. Did they ever sit down? Always ready to serve? Or always ready to murder?

Murder.

It returned as quickly as a squash ball hit by Detective Roger LeCarre from a wall. Here they were at the funeral for one murder and along came another. This one, somehow, was even more shocking and sudden than the last.

*Bang!*

LeCarre's ears rang. A piercing, throbbing sound reverberated around the chapel.

A dead bishop on the ground.

And a gun.

In LeCarre's hand.

With one bullet missing from its chamber.

# FOURTEEN

Back in the cupboard. Back in confinement, like a repeat offender, except one whose only offence was to keep getting locked away for murders he didn't do.

'I knew it!' Cynthia Pest had said. 'He bamboozled us with numbers, nonsense about his height and impact points and downward stabbing motions and whatnot, to win us over. But he did it! He killed Eli Quartz and then we let him out and he killed the Bishop! This murder was our fault! We're to blame!'

'The only person to blame is that ghastly man, LeCarre!' Patricia Beresford had said.

It hurt. To have the county's finest radio actress call you ghastly. *No one wanted that.* But this was where Detective Roger LeCarre found himself. Would he have done the same? Locked away the man holding the gun that fired the bullet? Surely he would? And yet, LeCarre hadn't fired the gun, he hadn't pulled the trigger, he *knew* he hadn't. LeCarre had always made a conscious effort to know what his fingers were doing at all times. It didn't make any sense.

LeCarre began to reassess his whole career. He had to. How many people had he arrested, had he convicted for this or that over the years? Hundreds? Thousands? It had to be thousands. Hundreds *and* thousands, sprinkled all over Devon and Cornwall. Surely, amongst that list, there had to have been a mistake or two. Something he missed. A seemingly cut-and-dried case, with some invisible clue he'd failed to see. A miscarriage of justice just like the one he was now the victim of.

No. He was Detective Roger LeCarre and he didn't get things wrong. That was what defined him. Even if the quizmaster at the Crown and Goose *said* his answer was wrong, even if the internet, every book on the subject, said his answer was wrong, Detective Roger LeCarre knew he was right. Why? Because he was Detective Roger LeCarre and Detective Roger LeCarre didn't get things wrong because Detective Roger LeCarre couldn't *afford* to get things wrong. It was true on quiz night at the Crown and Goose and it was true out on the streets. 'I can't afford to get things wrong!' he'd shout at the quizmaster, while they insisted to him that Canberra was the capital of Australia while LeCarre absolutely, positively *knew* it was Sydney. No. LeCarre was always right because he had to be. Every person behind bars thanks to Roger LeCarre was there because they deserved to be, and that was the end of it.

'Get in there and think about what you've done,' Peacock had said as he'd turned the key.

'I'll just get out through the trap door again, you know I will!'

'Not this time you won't. I've sealed them all. There's no escape.'

'I didn't do it, Peacock. Make sure you lock away the gun,' said LeCarre.

'Of course I'm locking it away. I should never have taken it out in the first place,' said Peacock.

Back in the cupboard. An ugly little space. Untidy, damp. A hidden blemish at Powderham. Vital to the running of the house, but tucked away, out of sight, the swan's feet under the water. Back in his cell. Immediately he regretted not emptying the bucket. Now he was sitting next to it again. A bucket of his own waste. I bet Mandela didn't have to deal with this, he thought to himself. LeCarre had been meaning to read Mandela's biography for years. If he'd known he'd spend so much of the weekend alone in a cupboard, he'd have brought a book.

LeCarre was a real man and therefore only read non-fiction. The worst genre, without a doubt, was crime fiction. To think that while LeCarre was out on the streets and cul-de-sacs, there were supposed novelists, sitting in their cosy houses, writing books that profited from the crime that LeCarre faced down every day. It was as if the whole thing was one big joke. Crime fiction made LeCarre sick.

Back in the clink. LeCarre had seen prison change people. For better or worse. Some went in petty criminals and came out masterminds. Some went in like remorseless slabs of evil and came out repenting choirboys. Would this new imprisonment change him? If the weather stayed as it was, he could be looking at a one- or two-day stretch. Perhaps he'd come out like Mike Tyson, converted to Islam and looking for a title fight.

LeCarre picked up his trusty ball and bounced it against the opposite wall.

*Ba dum pap. Ba dum pap. Ba dum pap.*

Patricia Beresford: She had a motive for killing Eli Quartz but not for killing the Bishop and not for framing LeCarre, as far as he could see. Perhaps she was researching the role of a serial killer and had fallen in too deep. You didn't get to give the kind of performances Beresford had for so many years on *Jam on Top* without serious dedication. Could she have 'gone method' and taken it too far? They'd had a serious problem with it in Cornwall for years. Actors would come down to stay at their holiday homes to work on their next role and end up going on a killing spree because they were so in character. In the end, Daniel Day Lewis was given a lifetime ban from the county.

LeCarre and the Bishop had overheard her too. 'Tired of living a lie. I love you', that's what she'd said. What lie? And to whom had she said it? There was no one else there. No phones were working.

LeCarre had been churning the words in his mind until he realised. She was an actor. Patricia Beresford had taken the opportunity of some alone time to run some lines. But for what? *Jam on Top* was over, the Quartz-funded tour was cancelled. A secret project?

*Ba dum pap. Ba dum pap. Ba dum pap.*

Anthony Little-Hope: the Professor. Another man who knew the castle. He was the country's foremost expert on Powderham. It was certainly credible to think he'd have strong opinions about an American taking over the earldom. Also, it was very hard to see him approving of what Quartz was doing to the castle. Disapproving enough to kill him? He didn't look like a killer. He looked like a nerd. Sure, nerds could be killers, but he was an unusual candidate. He looked like the kind of man who made a big batch of vegetable soup on a Sunday night and then ate it for lunch every day that week. Not the type who murdered two people in less than twenty-four hours. He'd said something about Eli Quartz donating to his department at Exeter University. Surely that would be a man you'd want to keep alive?

One could imagine a university academic opposing organised religion. There was an Exeter University quiz team at the Crown and Goose, full of smug professors in jumpers, drinking orange juice and ordering halloumi burgers and mumbling about their latest gender. They all thought they were smarter than God. That was, until the sports round came up and it all fell apart. It was easy to see a university professor not liking the police too. LeCarre had seen them at their filthy protests, waving their filthy placards. They were all lefty pinkos who saw the police as the enforcement arm of an evil state. If you drove a car anyone would want to steal, then you'd need us, LeCarre would think to himself. Framing a police officer for a crime – Little-Hope might see it as some kind of poetic justice, LeCarre supposed. Professors loved poetry.

LeCarre had found a lot of motives but not a lot of methods. It was hard to see how the killer was doing all of this. He almost admired them. Twice someone had died and twice he'd been caught with the murder weapon in his hand. He couldn't admire a murderer, though. That would be sick. Nurses, that's who LeCarre admired. Nurses and Paralympians and Captain Tom and sick kids singing songs on *Britain's Got Talent*. That was who LeCarre admired. Not murderers.

*Ba dum pap. Ba dum pap. Ba dum pap.*

Cynthia Pest: the Duchess seemed permanently on edge. LeCarre had supposed that that was the cocaine leaving her system, that she hadn't brought enough with her to support her habit through a snowstorm. But maybe it was all the murdering she was doing. Murder does have a habit of making people twitchy, especially the people doing it.

Pest, for all LeCarre knew, could be in some wild drug-induced frenzy. Her addled mind thought she was slaying dragons and not billionaires and bishops. But she was so slight. Either the murder methods somehow required no force from the perpetrator, or she was in cahoots. But with who? She hardly seemed like the most popular attendee. Also, the framing of LeCarre – that would take a clarity of thought unlikely to be found in a junkie, however regal.

The Duchess of Totnes could well have an unfavourable opinion on the new Earl of Devon. In fact, she *did* and hadn't been shy about expressing it. She was a true royal, one with centuries of royal blood flowing through her veins. One could imagine her thinking nothing of shedding the blood of an imposter like Eli Quartz.

And there was the matter of her strong reaction to Quartz's big game hunting. Some people cared more for animals than they did humans and Cynthia Pest appeared to be one such person. LeCarre had no sympathy with the sentiment. 'Come back to me the day one can put together an Ikea wardrobe,' he'd say whenever his wife brought up the subject of animal rights. Pest's motives for killing the Bishop and framing LeCarre were less apparent, but that didn't mean that they didn't exist.

*Ba dum pap. Ba dum pap. Ba dum pap.*

The Peacocks: Arthur and Angela. They could have done it as a duo. They knew the castle better than anyone and they'd known Quartz long enough to develop a hatred.

The Peacocks had worked for the old Earl of Devon, a man LeCarre knew nothing of. Where was he? How did he come to sell his title? There was so much LeCarre didn't know. What he did swirled around in his mind like numbered ping-pong balls in a tombola.

One thing was for sure – he had to get out of this cupboard. And then came his chance.

'Argh! Arrrrrgh!'

A woman's voice from outside, a strangled shriek, followed by a thud on the ground.

'Oh my God, she's not breathing!' LeCarre heard Angela Peacock say.

'Cold water. I'll get cold water,' said Arthur Peacock.

'What happened? She's turning blue!' said Pest.

'CPR!' yelled Little-Hope. 'Does anyone know CPR? Someone must know CPR!'

'I do,' said LeCarre, from inside the cupboard.

# FIFTEEN

LeCarre would never forget the time he learned CPR, or cardiopulmonary resuscitation to give it its full name. He had an argument with the instructor on the day. 'Cardiopulmonary is one word so surely it should be CR. As an abbreviation, it just doesn't work.'

'It's a universally understood abbreviation,' they'd said. 'Anyway, I don't really think it's the important detail.'

'When you're a detective, you learn that *all* details are important. But if you're seriously happy using CPR as your abbreviation then, by all means, carry on.'

Chief Superintendent Beverley Chang had booked the whole station in for a lesson. LeCarre was no fan of courses. The only course he was interested in going on was Silverstone, powering around every corner in his Kia Ceed, staying within the legal speed limit at all times because he didn't want to fall into any bad habits. But he'd taken part, to be a team player, and just three months later it had saved his own life when he'd had a heart attack and performed CPR on himself.

CPR on himself? Doesn't seem likely, does it? Well, it happened. Most people don't possess that kind of inner strength. The kind required to perform CPR on yourself. Luckily for Detective Roger LeCarre, he did. He'd stumbled out of the Crown and Goose after another night of heavy drinking and found himself on the pavement going into cardiac arrest. I like arrests, he'd thought to himself. But not this kind. With his lifestyle, a heart attack had always been on the cards. Some men burn the candle at both ends; LeCarre set fire to the whole thing.

On his back and with no one around, LeCarre knew he was the only man who could save himself. He thought back to the course. Firm chest compressions at a rate of 100 to 120 a minute. He dragged his own arms up and did exactly that, pounding his own chest, summoning strength from somewhere deep, deep down inside his crooked soul. It took a full ten minutes for him to bring himself back to life, but he did it. When he'd told people the next day, they hadn't believed him. 'Do you not think that maybe you just had a bit too much to drink and fell over?'

'No. I had a heart attack and brought myself back to life by giving myself CPR. You weren't there!'

And now here he was, doing CPR again, saving another life, but this time not his own. This time Patricia Beresford.

'One, two, three, four, five, six . . . '

'Can you stop doing that, please?' LeCarre said to Little-Hope. 'It's easier if I count myself.'

'Sorry.'

Thirty compressions and then mouth to mouth. This wasn't the first actress he'd kissed, but it was the first he'd given the kiss of life.

'Don't die on me, Patricia!' he said dramatically. 'Devon loves you. Don't die on me!'

A county couldn't lose its earl, its bishop and its most beloved radio actress in one weekend. That kind of grief a county would find it difficult to recover from. LeCarre could picture it: a whole county closing its curtains, crawling into bed and fading away.

Thirty more compressions. Then his lips to hers again. Those lips he knew so well. Not because he'd touched them before but because they had touched him, with the words they'd spoken as Thelma Bertwhistle. Every county had its shining light, its reason to get up in the morning. Norfolk had Delia Smith. Lancashire had Vernon Kay. None shone so bright as Patricia Beresford. He felt her Devon breath exhale, saw her eyes refocus on the world, felt her pulse return.

'You gave us quite the fright there, Ms Beresford,' said LeCarre, like the reluctant hero he was.

Patricia Beresford wasn't yet ready to talk.

'Dear God,' said Pest. 'What a weekend!'

LeCarre felt a familiar taste on his tongue. What was it?

'I do beg your pardon, Ms Beresford. There's something I have to check.' He kissed her again. This time with passion, scraping the inside of her mouth with his tongue. She reciprocated. Having just nearly died, she wasn't really in the mood, but when Detective Roger LeCarre kisses you, you take your chance.

'I hardly think this is the time,' said Arthur Peacock, disapprovingly.

LeCarre licked his own lips in concentration.

'My suspicions were correct,' said LeCarre. 'I'm afraid to say that this was no accident. Ms Beresford was poisoned.'

The group agreed, with some hesitance, that LeCarre should be allowed to stay out of the cupboard. It was decided that,

on balance, there was too much doubt to keep him imprisoned, especially considering he could be the man who
saved any one of them – the man who caught the killer. It
seemed clear that he hadn't been the person who attempted
to kill Beresford, seeing as he'd been locked away and had
come out to save her. That put all previous assumptions
about him murdering Quartz and the Bishop under review.
It was just too unbelievable that a police officer would so
blatantly murder them and then deny it. Something else
was going on.

Angela Peacock had hugged him in relief.

'I thought she was ... I thought she was going to die!
Right there on the floor!'

'She's all right now,' LeCarre had whispered softly in her
sexy ear. 'There, there. She's all right now.'

The touch of a woman. It had been nearly twenty-four
hours since the last time he'd had intercourse. He needed
to get back to Carrie. This year he'd vowed to be faithful.
Six days in and, except for a small slip-up at his squash club,
he'd kept to his promise.


A new, uneasy atmosphere pervaded the castle. All but the
killer knew nothing. Only that their lives were in immediate danger. They found themselves gathered, organically,

in the music room, chairs facing the rose garden in a kind of horseshoe, watching the vicious weather. Each drank tea, each cup made by the person who drank it, each made with meticulous caution. There was a poisoner amongst them, after all.

In the quiet, reality sank in. It was Saturday afternoon. They were here until at least morning. *Any one of them could be next.*

The snow was deeper than the last time anyone had looked. They were more trapped than ever. An expanse of white. Whiter than anything any of them had ever seen, whiter than a Totnes farmers market, whiter than the cast of *Jam on Top*. The expertly pruned hedges suffered from the weight of snow that sat on top, like a weight on its shoulders, the weight they all felt.

'*Football Focus* should be on about now,' said LeCarre.

They were just eight miles from Exeter, eight miles from civilisation, but they might as well have been on the moon. No internet, no communications, no way out. Strangers thrown together to endure it. It was if they were contestants on *Celebrity Big Brother* except, instead of getting evicted, you got murdered.

Snow continued to tumble from the sky like a billion tiny paratroopers, wind battering the flakes into the giant floor-to-ceiling windows, providing the only sound other than sporadic slurps of tea and LeCarre's *Football Focus* comment. Everyone was waiting. Waiting for the weather to clear, or the murderer to strike again – whichever came first. It was hard to believe they'd finished their evil work. Murder was like Pringles – very more-ish: once you popped you couldn't stop.

LeCarre would begin interrogations soon. Each suspect had to be questioned. It was only fair that they had this moment of quiet, though. They'd all been through so much already. They'd seen two men murdered, two men from entirely different worlds, who now lay side by side in the chapel.

Through the snow, very little was clear. The outline of some trees, perhaps a boat on the water, or maybe it was a massive cow. Hard to tell. LeCarre squinted.

'What's that?'

'What's what?' said Pest.

'There's a building of some sort,' said LeCarre.

'A building?' said Beresford. 'I thought there was nothing between here and the river.'

'No, I can see it. Is that a turret?' said LeCarre.

'That'll be the Belvedere,' said Arthur Peacock.

'The Belvedere?' said LeCarre.

'The Belvedere Tower,' said Anthony Little-Hope. 'It's on the grounds. The old family used to use it for entertainment. Centuries ago. It had a little ballroom. It's derelict now, I believe. Is that right, Mr Peacock?'

'Yes, sir. Completely derelict. Nearly burned down after the war.'

'A ballroom?' Pest sighed. 'Weren't we promised a party? This was supposed to be a party. It's anything but. If this is a party, then I'm a manual labourer.'

'I suppose we could have a party,' said Beresford. 'I did bring a selection of gowns.'

'It hardly seems appropriate, don't you think?' said Little-Hope.

'Oh, don't be such a stick-in-the-mud,' said Beresford.

'Peacock, the Belvedere Tower?' said Little-Hope.

'Yes, sir.'

'Am I correct in thinking that it has a bell?'

'That's right, sir.'

'Yes, that's right. The bell!' said Little-Hope. 'In the seventeenth century, when somebody died in the village, the family at Powderham would ring the bell, a sort of ancient "breaking news", if you will. Hasn't been rung for centuries, I expect.'

If this were a novel, LeCarre thought, that bell would be

the sort of thing that would return somewhere later in the story. But this wasn't a book. This was real life and he had some interrogating to do.

# SIXTEEN

'Step into my office, Mr Peacock,' said Detective Roger LeCarre, leaning back in an Edwardian chair. 'Please take a seat.'

The library wasn't a library any more. It was a colony of Exeter Police Station. It was Detective Roger LeCarre's interrogation room. If interrogation was an art form then Roger LeCarre was its Leonardo da Vinci, its Claude Monet, its Pablo Picasso and – what's that woman one? – its Tracey Emin, all rolled into one. His mouth was his paintbrush, his words were his paint and, right now, Arthur Peacock would be his canvas. Interrogation was about teasing answers out of people, not bludgeoning them, and LeCarre was one of the old masters. He'd take this slowly.

Peacock sat down.

'Can I get you a drink, Mr Peacock?' asked LeCarre, turning to a globe which, when the top was lifted, revealed itself to be a bar.

'No, thank you, sir. I'm more comfortable serving the drinks, sir, I have to say.'

'Yes, you are comfortable serving drinks, aren't you, Mr Peacock?' said LeCarre, taking an intelligent sip of brandy. 'But are you also comfortable serving *murder*? Murder, Mr Peacock? I'm sure you've heard of it. Ever done it? *Murder?* Murder anyone this weekend, did you, by any chance, Mr Peacock? Murder two people, did you, Mr Peacock? Or should I call you Mr Murderer? Is that your real name, Mr Peacock? Mr Murderer? Because you like to murder so much?'

'I didn't kill Eli Quartz, Detective, and I didn't kill the Bishop.'

'Here's the thing, Mr Peacock. I've been in this business a long time and, you see, that's just the sort of thing a murderer would say.'

LeCarre took an old book from a shelf and casually flicked through its pages.

'Do you read books, Mr Peacock?'

'Not really, sir. Don't get the time. Taking care of the house keeps me busy.'

The Lee Childs on Peacock's bedside table. He had the

time. If Arthur Peacock was prepared to lie about that, what else was he prepared to lie about? LeCarre slammed the book down on a table beside him, leaned in and hit Peacock with a killer line.

*'I read people.'*

Peacock blinked. Perhaps with nerves, perhaps just because he needed to blink. It was difficult to tell at this stage.

'You didn't like Eli Quartz very much, did you, Mr Peacock?'

'He was my master. How I felt about him didn't come into it.'

'Oh, I find that hard to believe, Mr Peacock,' said LeCarre, taking another, even more intelligent, sip of brandy.

'You obviously don't understand what it means to be a butler, Detective. You have pride in your job, don't you, Detective? *Don't you?* You may not have liked his lordship yourself. But you're still investigating his murder because you're a detective and that's your job. You want to do a good job, Detective, at least I hope you do. I'm no different. You see ...'

Now Peacock leaned in to deliver *his* killer line, meaning that the men's faces were so close that it was a bit weird, actually.

'*I'm a butler.* My father was a butler. His father was a butler. His father before him was a butler. His father was a butler. *His* father was a butler. Then his father was a website developer but his father? Butler. And his father before him was a butler. Then his father was a butler. *His* father worked in the fishing industry for a while but then he was a butler. *His* father? Butler. And his father before him was a butler. His father was a butler ...'

'Sorry, how far are you intending to go back? I'm getting the general idea,' said LeCarre.

'The Peacocks are butlers. It's what we do. We look after our masters. It's not our job to have an opinion on them.'

'What time did you go to bed last night, Mr Peacock?'

'About 10.30, I expect, sir.'

'And did you go straight to sleep?'

'No, it was Friday night, so I watched the popular chat show with Graham Norton on BBC One. To unwind, you know. It's not a crime to unwind, is it?'

That depends, thought LeCarre. Some men unwind with a packet of spliffs.

'Didn't get up at all in the night, did you, Mr Peacock? I heard footsteps on the stairs. Rearranging evidence, were you?'

'No, sir.'

Then LeCarre thought of a question so good that he decided to reposition himself in order to deliver it. He stood up and faced the bookshelves, running his finger along the spines like an osteopath – an osteopath of books.

'And tell me, Mr Peacock . . . ' LeCarre turned 180 degrees and fired his next question at the butler like an inquisitive arrow. 'Who were the guests on *Graham Norton* last night?'

'Sir Kenneth Branagh, Salma Hayek and Devon's very own Josh Widdicombe.'

Peacock was dead on. LeCarre had always made a point of learning that week's guests on *Graham Norton* in case it came up in an investigation.

'You rattled off those names rather quick, Mr Peacock. Almost as if you learned them.'

'It was a good episode, Detective. The fascinating yet sincere contributions of Branagh and Hayek were nicely counterbalanced by Widdicombe's irreverent wit.'

'I see. And who was the musical guest?'

'Give me a moment, yes, that's right – Ellie Goulding.'

LeCarre paused. Every case is a jigsaw without a picture on its box. You don't know what it is until all the pieces are in the right place. LeCarre wondered whether he even had the right pieces. Perhaps some of them had been hoovered up. Sometimes you had to open up the vacuum cleaner and dig into the hoover bag. That could be an unpleasant job. Not that LeCarre had ever done it before. Carrie tended to do the cleaning, except for a brief period where they'd hired a cleaner, but that didn't work out in the end because LeCarre caught her leaving the house with one of their sponges and arrested her.

'You heard footsteps?'

LeCarre nodded.

'What makes you think that the killer is from this world, Detective LeCarre?'

'What do you mean?'

Now it was Arthur Peacock's turn to stand up and look at the bookshelves in a dramatic yet entirely unnecessary fashion.

'I'm talking about the spirit world, Detective.'

LeCarre's eyebrows rose roughly half a centimetre each.

'Do you mean, like, ghosts and that?'

Peacock turned to face LeCarre, his bald head shimmering in the halogen light.

'Ever heard of the Grey Lady?'

# SEVENTEEN

Detective Roger LeCarre's mind fought new battles every day, grappling with problems, the likes of which might cripple a lesser man. How can one human hurt another? How does one find peace in an evil world? What's the best time of day to avoid traffic on the Tamar Bridge? Now a new question had landed in his troubled inbox – how does one apprehend an apparition?

LeCarre was a man of logic. Ghosts didn't exist. *They couldn't.* Surely it would have been in the news or something. And yet, given the peculiar manner in which Quartz and the Bishop had died – with LeCarre holding the murder weapon – maybe the explanation LeCarre was searching for *did* lie in the supernatural.

'She be a wispy figure. A spectre that walks the halls at night,' Peacock said, mystically. 'Legend says she was the wife of the first earl. No one knows how she died but they say it were murder. Now she comes looking for revenge.'

'The Grey Lady, you say?'

'Grey. So grey. As grey as the Devon sky on a winter's day, as grey as a sheet from a bubble-jet printer running out of ink. So grey.'

'You've seen her?'

'With my own two eyes.'

LeCarre counted Arthur Peacock's eyes. He did indeed have two – his story seemed to stand up. Were circumstances anything close to normal, LeCarre would now go about consulting an expert in the paranormal, but such a course of action wasn't available. He was stuck. He couldn't even access the internet. He'd have to research the paranormal in the old-fashioned way, by consulting the most reliable expert he'd ever known – *his own brain*.

So what did he know? Spooky. Ghosts were spooky. *Really* spooky. They haunted stuff. Old places like ... like ... castles! They haunted castles! Castles and old manor houses! They were in a castle/manor house now! Good. He was getting somewhere.

There was a trend seeping its way into the police service, a new respect for academia: recruits with degrees from fancy universities, consultants with doctorates in criminology. The way LeCarre saw it, there was no substitute for the kind of common-sense investigative techniques he was using right now – thinking about how spooky ghosts were and wondering whether their ability to walk through walls could help them to murder.

LeCarre had never seen a ghost. At least he didn't think he had. Sometimes, walking down a high street he'd see faded shop signs, the remnants of an old Woolworth's or a long-shut BHS. But they were another kind of ghost, ghosts of his childhood, ghosts of a past that would never come back to Devon. A time when Britain was a country he understood, when high street retail was solid and dependable, as solid as the streets on which those iconic shops stood, like cultural landmarks offering pick and mix and reasonable returns policies. But that wasn't the kind of ghost he was dealing with now. No, now he was dealing with a ghost in an old castle, murdering people with elephant tusks and stuff.

'What does she look like, this Grey Lady?' asked LeCarre.

'If I told you, you wouldn't believe me,' said Peacock.

'Try me.'

'Spine-chilling! Long, wispy hair, covers most of her face. She wears a nightgown that ripples in the draught that seems to follow her wherever she goes. She moves slowly, but she does not walk. It's as if she glides across the floor. In her hand she holds a candle . . . '

'To be honest, she sounds pretty much like a standard ghost to me,' said LeCarre. 'Have you ever spoken to her?'

'Never. I've never heard her speak, but . . . ' Peacock's eyes narrowed and stared into a middle distance, displaying a sinister truth that seemed to haunt him. 'I know she doesn't want us here.'

'How do you know that, Mr Peacock?'

'Because of all the terrible things that have happened to us. The Grey Lady, she's responsible. I know it.'

LeCarre hadn't failed to notice that there was no Mrs Peacock.

'Your wife. Angela's mother?' LeCarre slipped into an empathetic tone. 'What happened to her, Mr Peacock?'

'They say she jumped.'

'Jumped? What's wrong with that? People jump all the . . . oh, do you mean, like, off a building?'

'From our bedroom window,' said Peacock, tears in his butler eyes. 'I know she was sad – she didn't jump, though. She was pushed.'

'By the Grey Lady?'

'That's what I think, Detective,' said Peacock.

'Why was she sad?' asked LeCarre. 'Your wife. What was her name?'

'Rihanna.'

'Not *the* Rihanna?'

'No, different one.'

'Right, thought so. That would have been mental. Why was Rihanna sad?'

'Because of our son,' said Peacock, whose eyes were now two small puddles, balanced on his face.

'Your son? You have a son?' said LeCarre.

'He was taken away from us.'

*The empty spare room in the servants' quarters.*

LeCarre shifted in his seat. In a moment, he'd turned from interrogator to counsellor. This was the life of a Devon and Cornwall police officer. You had to be all things to all men. Everyone you spoke to seemed to be in some kind of pain. He felt like a physiotherapist.

'What happened?' asked LeCarre, softening his voice, like it was a tub of Häagen-Dazs on a radiator.

Peacock took a hankie from his breast pocket and wiped his eyes.

'Peter was supposed to follow in my footsteps and become

a butler. He would have run this home when I retired. He would have been good at it too, I know he would. Being a butler isn't easy, Detective, but he had what it took. Then he got distracted.'

'Distracted?' said LeCarre, repeating the last word Peacock had said and putting a question mark at the end.

'I blame Freeview. Powderham Castle is a very stable place, Detective. It's hardly changed in six hundred years, at least until Mr Quartz came along, but that was after Peter left. It was Freeview that did it. As soon as he started watching channels like Quest and Challenge TV and 5USA, he started talking different. Saying there was more to life than being a butler. Saying there was a whole world out there that he wanted to explore. Crazy talk! That's when he started going to . . . ' Peacock clenched his fist and tensed his jaw. '*Exeter.*'

Peacock said the proper noun as if it were the source of all evil, and maybe it was. At least all East Devon evil, anyway. The Exeter mafia still controlled all Devon crime east of Dartmoor. LeCarre could see why a man living in the relative sanctuary of Powderham Castle wouldn't want their son dipping his toes into Exeter's criminal waters.

'That city,' spat Peacock. 'It just swallowed him up. "I'm

just off to Cineworld, Dad," he'd say. Or, "I'm just popping into town, Dad. The new Richard Osman is in stock at Waterstones." His mother was worried but I said, "He needs his independence, you know. It's just a phase." I should have listened to her.'

'And now he's no longer with us?' said LeCarre.

'Gone. An evil bastard took him away from us.'

LeCarre tried to recall the name. Peter Peacock. Maybe he'd investigated his murder. So many names, so many murders, it was hard to remember them all. LeCarre saw more bodies than a Turkish bath.

'And Rihanna, she . . . ?'

'She took it very badly,' said Peacock.

'Sorry, we're talking about your wife now, right? Not the singer?'

'Yes, Rihanna Peacock took it very badly. But she wouldn't have killed herself. That wasn't the Rihanna I knew. It was the Grey Lady. I know it.'

LeCarre's mind turned to Peacock's extraordinarily attractive daughter, but not in a creepy way.

'And Angela?'

'Angela? What about Angela?' said Peacock defensively, his body suddenly ready for a fight.

'How has she coped?'

'She's fine! She's absolutely fine. As long as she stays at Powderham she's fine,' said Peacock.

'You won't let her leave?' said LeCarre.

'She can leave any time she likes. Except today, due to the fact that we're currently trapped because of the weather. But Angela would never want to leave Powderham. She's a clever girl. She knows there's nothing for her out there.'

It seemed a tragedy that the world would never get to see Angela's beauty, but LeCarre could understand Arthur Peacock's determination to keep her at Powderham. He'd already lost a son and a wife. Some of the world's wonders were hidden away for centuries. In finding Angela, LeCarre felt like an explorer turning a corner in Jordan and stumbling upon Petra. He felt privileged to have met her now, while she was still a secret, before she became a tourist attraction with daily visiting coach parties and a gift shop. Given the option, LeCarre would buy a season ticket to stand and stare at Angela Peacock, and he was sure millions of others would do the same. Perhaps it was best for everyone that such a situation was avoided. Especially considering LeCarre's longstanding and vociferous opposition to the objectification of women.

LeCarre looked at Arthur Peacock. The lines on his face

told a story. Lines on faces always told stories. Maybe one day, after he retired, LeCarre would open a bookshop that instead of selling books, sold the lines on people's faces – those were the best stories of all. Arthur Peacock's lines told the story of a man who loved his family.

'Well, thank you for your time, Mr Peacock,' said LeCarre. 'You've been very helpful.'

'Will that be all, sir?'

'For now, I think, yes,' said LeCarre.

Peacock got up to leave, once again adopting the military-like posture of an upright servant.

'Oh, one more thing, Mr Peacock?' said LeCarre.

Peacock turned back to face LeCarre.

'How many tusks do elephants have?'

'Two, sir.'

'Yes, I thought so. Then we're missing a tusk. Do you know where that might be?'

'I don't know, sir. I never saw it. Maybe Mr Quartz never had them both shipped over. Or he could have kept that one at one of his other houses. If it was at Powderham, I expect it's in his study.'

'His study?' said LeCarre. 'I don't think we saw that on the tour. Where is it?'

'It's just behind you, sir.'

LeCarre turned. All he could see was a bookshelf.

'Push,' said Peacock.

LeCarre put the palm of his hand to a row of books and pushed.

# EIGHTEEN

Detective Roger LeCarre elegantly entered the room through the time-honoured method of walking through a door. A secret door. He left Peacock behind. Peacock was still a suspect, one who could use this as an opportunity to tamper with evidence in the study. LeCarre had to do this alone.

If Powderham Castle was another world, one far, far away from the ghettos of Devon, then Eli Quartz's study was a world within that world – a world within a world within a world. How many more layers would LeCarre have to peel back before he got to the truth?

LeCarre was tired. No wonder Mandela had only lasted five years as president of South Africa after his release from prison. Just one night in a cupboard and LeCarre felt like he needed a pint of elderflower cordial and a lie-down. But he couldn't lie down. Not until he'd solved the murders. Or at least until after 10 p.m., otherwise he'd completely mess up his sleep pattern.

LeCarre slowly rotated his body a full 360 degrees and took in his surroundings. The room was a kind of centaur – half one thing, half another – half office, half playpen to a billionaire bachelor. This was a dead man's playpen now. Much of what LeCarre assumed were old features of the house remained – wood-panelled walls, another marble fireplace, a large mahogany desk made by Chippendale or possibly Oak Furnitureland, LeCarre wasn't sure. But there were signs of the modern man who'd purchased Powderham too. On the desk sat a change jar full of Bitcoins.

Behind the desk, embedded into the wall, was a tropical fish tank. This had to have been a Quartz addition, seeing as at the time the castle was built, tropical fish weren't invented yet, although once he had internet reception again, LeCarre would double-check that fact on his phone.

LeCarre's eyes followed one neon blue and yellow fish as it made its way around the elaborate paradise of a home that had been created for it inside its tank. More care had gone into his home than into most homes in West Side, Exeter, thought LeCarre.

'Who killed your daddy, little fishy?' said LeCarre, pointlessly.

Hung up on the walls were paintings. Some, most likely, of former residents of the castle, seated proudly on horses, or simply standing to attention in naval gear. Then, in the same neoclassical style, paintings of Eli Quartz on a quad bike or holding an AR-15. He was clearly trying to position himself as the next in a long line of great men, but something didn't fit.

No matter how much money you had, you couldn't buy class. Some men had it, some men didn't. LeCarre had it in abundance. His tuxedo may have been wrinkled, his hair unkempt, after a night in the cupboard. But it didn't matter. Class oozed out of him, like juice out of an overripe pear.

No sign of any tusk. LeCarre had figured that if the tusk he was holding hadn't done the deed then perhaps the second one had. The murderer could have somehow cleaned it and neatly placed it back in the office while LeCarre was locked in the cupboard. It wasn't there, though, as far as LeCarre could see.

What was there were a number of prototypes, presumably for future Quartz Industries products. What Eli Quartz lacked in class, he made up for in brain power. LeCarre hardly knew what he was looking at. Half-finished oddities, boxes of screws and wires, a pair of boots with springs attached to their soles. Without thinking, LeCarre pressed a button on one contraption and then watched in amazement as four robot arms proceeded to make him a mojito. He took a sip. It tasted good. Damn, it tasted good. LeCarre sat in a leather chair, pressed a button on another device and suddenly his head was receiving a perfect haircut. Excited by what he was finding, LeCarre picked up another device, pressed another button and then watched in amazement as a TV came on. For a brief second he thought that was the best invention of all until he realised that, thinking about it, it was actually just a TV remote and he had about four of them at home.

LeCarre's mind was bamboozled by Quartz's genius. LeCarre would have liked to have got to know him better. Being one of Devon's only geniuses could get lonely. It was nice to have another one come along, but now Quartz was dead.

Could he have faked his own death? LeCarre certainly couldn't rule it out. What the motive was wasn't clear, but surely Quartz had the smarts and the means to do so? Such a man could have replaced himself with a fake corpse, escaped through a trap door and disappeared. No one could beat this weather, though, surely, however smart they were. For all

LeCarre knew, Quartz was hiding in some secluded corner of the house now, waiting to kill them all, one by one. But then, the search had revealed no one.

LeCarre had left the group alone. When he returned, would he find more mayhem? More bodies? *Dead* bodies? Dead *murdered* bodies? He had to move but something deep, deep inside his copper core was dragging him back towards the desk.

Ghosts, faked deaths, angry butlers, vengeful actresses – all of LeCarre's theories were about to be overtaken by a new piece of information lying dormant in Quartz's desk drawer. He pulled at the handle, delicately opening the drawer as if it were a woman's blouse. What he found inside was more momentous than the contents of any undergarment.

What he found inside blew the whole damn case wide open.

# NINETEEN

*Tick. Tock. Tick. Tock. Tick. Tock.* The sound of an eight-foot-high grandfather clock in the music room at Powderham Castle. The sound of time. Time marching on, bringing each guest closer to the moment they could leave. Or closer to death. Whichever came first.

Detective Roger LeCarre looked at the playing cards in his hand and couldn't bring himself to care. Those weren't the cards he was thinking about. He was thinking about the cards in the breast pocket of his crumpled dinner jacket. New cards. New cards that came not in the form of actual cards but in the form of a will, the will of Eli Jefferson Quartz. LeCarre had to choose the right time to play *these* cards very carefully. They were sure to cause a scene.

The guests had decided to pass the time with a game of gin rummy. Arthur and Angela Peacock had joined them. The lines between servant and served were fading away. These were unusual times. They were all in the same boat now, a boat that was sinking, a boat with no life jackets – a boat with a murderer at the helm.

'Rummy!' said LeCarre, slamming down his cards onto the Georgian card table.

'My goodness, that's the eleventh game you've won in a row,' said Cynthia Pest, who was somehow keeping it together in the midst of what appeared to be an enforced detox.

'What can I say? I'm a winner. Winning is what I do,' said LeCarre with typical humility.

Looking at Pest, he noticed that she no longer seemed quite so on edge. Was the need for cocaine already dissipating? Or had she somehow got hold of some? *Cocaine.* LeCarre said the filthy word in his own head. He hated it with a vengeance. It was without a doubt his least favourite white powder. Detergent, talc, even dandruff was better than cocaine, and a damn sight cheaper too.

'Are you going to be interrogating all of us, Detective?' asked Patricia Beresford. 'I have to say, I was rather looking forward to it.'

'Change of plan,' said LeCarre.

'Oh really?' said Beresford. 'How disappointing. Of course, your clever questions wouldn't work on me. I've been interrogated by the best of them, you know. *Woman's Weekly* magazine, BBC *Spotlight*, Kelly and Baz on the Radio Exe breakfast show *Up With Kelly and Baz*. You can ask me anything, anything at all, although I'd appreciate it if we steered clear of my love life. Everyone wants to know about my love life. The answer's always the same. I'm in love with one thing and one thing only. Entertaining people!'

'Why the change of plan?' asked Angela, sexily.

'Yes, Detective, why the change of plan?' said Anthony Little-Hope.

'Some new information has come to light,' said LeCarre.

'Oh really? How exciting!' said Beresford. 'What is it? Have you figured out who the murderer is? Let me guess. Reverend Green in the billiard room with the lead pipe!' Patricia Beresford erupted in laughter at her own joke. 'People say I can't do comedy but, you see, I can! I really can!'

'Well, come on, then,' said Little-Hope. 'Are you going to tell us? Or will it compromise your case to reveal it now? You're the expert. I wouldn't want to tread on your toes.'

LeCarre had a decision to make. Fine. Making decisions was what he did. What to have for breakfast (bran flakes, always bran flakes), what to wear (leather jacket and brown brogues), what radio station to listen to in the car (Radio Exe). But those decisions were easy. This one could have enormous consequences. If he broadcast his new information to the room now, the killer could do something unpredictable. Lives could be in danger. But it did present LeCarre with an opportunity. Revealing it here and now, in front of the whole group, gave LeCarre the chance to monitor everyone's reaction. How they each responded to the news could be very telling.

'Personally, I think we should wait until the police get here. Once we're able to contact them, that is,' said Cynthia Pest. 'I'm sure they can handle everything properly.'

LeCarre leaned in, like a feminist woman looking for a promotion.

*'I am the police.'*

And with that, he took a piece of paper from his breast pocket.

'This, ladies and gentlemen, is the last will and testament of Eli Jefferson Quartz.'

'Oh goodness,' said Angela, putting her hand to her beautiful mouth.

'Surely this doesn't concern any of us?' said Pest. 'We hardly knew the man.'

'Well, I knew him a little. He was funding my tour, after all,' said Beresford.

'*Was* funding,' said Little-Hope. 'He was pulling out of that, if I remember correctly. In fact, I seem to recall you being rather upset, Ms Beresford.'

'Yes, but ... but ... perhaps he had bigger plans for me. Oh, dear God, I've lived a life on radio money, silly pathetic little regional radio money. You don't know how hard it's been for me. Having a whole county recognise my voice, living my life in the public ear and not being properly rewarded for it. A semi-detached, that's what I live in. A four-bedroom semi in Heavitree. It's hell! Of course, I wasn't always known. People don't know how much I've struggled. All the odd jobs I had to do in the early days to get by. I used to nanny, looking after the little squirts of the aristocracy. Do you know how I got my Equity card? I became a stage hypnotist. I'm a serious actress. Making drunken idiots in holiday camps think they were chickens for moronic audiences. It was humiliating! I deserve this. I really do. Finally God has seen fit to turn His gaze to little old, six-time Devon Radio Actress of the Year Patricia Beresford. How much? No, don't tell me. How much? Obviously, not everything. He'd have had family, I'm sure. Just a gesture, I expect. But the man was worth billions, wasn't he? Oh my goodness, billions! He'd obviously taken a shine to me. I'm sure he left me something. £500 million. That would be nothing to him. £500 million?! I promise it won't change me, I really do. Of course, I suppose, it's not necessarily money, is it? Property? Not Powderham? Powderham! I suppose it would be fitting for the Queen of Devon to reside in the county's finest manor. Oh, Eli. What a wonderful man you were. Arthur! Angela! I promise to treat you both with respect at all times, although I will be asking you to reapply for your jobs. It's important to me that I do everything I can to return Powderham Castle to its former glory. If that means making a few changes, then so be it. I have a responsibility now, as Lady of the Manor, and I intend to take it very seriously. Now, the rose garden, what if we were to turn it into more of a—'

'"This is the final will and testament of Eli Jefferson Quartz . . ."' For once the ears of Devon, or at least those at Powderham Castle, were turned not to Patricia Beresford but to Detective Roger LeCarre. '"I, Eli Jefferson Quartz, a resident of Devon, United Kingdom, being of sound mind and body, do hereby henceforth thereof state the following.

All of my assets, liquid or otherwise, I do leave in their entirety to the History Department at Exeter University."'

The change was rapid. Suddenly every face in the room, every eye, every ear, every body, every hair, was pointed towards Professor Anthony Little-Hope as if they had instantly converted to Islam and he was their Mecca – except they weren't pointed in worship, they were pointed in shock. Were they pointed towards a murderer?

'Oh my!' said Little-Hope.

LeCarre continued. '"All of my holdings in Quartz Industries and future royalties from Quartz Industries, I do leave in their entirety to the History Department at Exeter University. All of my properties, both foreign and domestic, including Powderham Castle, I do leave in their entirety to the History Department at Exeter University."'

'You bastard!' Arthur Peacock had Little-Hope by the throat and against the blueish-green wall, his feet six inches above the ground.

'Let him go,' said LeCarre.

'He's a murderer!' said Peacock. 'He murdered Mr Quartz. He murdered the Bishop. He tried to murder Ms Beresford. He could murder any one of us next. Any one of us!'

'Let. Him. Go,' said LeCarre, using his Supernanny voice for the third time that day.

Peacock did as he was told, letting Little-Hope drop to the ground like a sack of educated potatoes in a corduroy suit. Little-Hope whimpered, arse on the floor, arms wrapped around his academic knees. LeCarre had seen it many times before. Criminals who crumbled into blubbering wrecks as soon as they were confronted with their actions.

'I didn't do it. You have to believe me!' said Little-Hope.

'I don't have to believe a goddamn thing,' said LeCarre. 'This is the problem with you professors. You're always telling us what to believe. What not to believe. Acid rain, climate change, photosynthesis. It's just a bunch of theories. But unless we subscribe to your thesis, we're cast as idiots. Well, I've been in the policing business for long enough to know that there's nothing more idiotic than murder. You know what I believe in, Professor? I believe in the Devon and Cornwall police force, I believe in something called chem trails, but we can talk about that another time, and I believe in my gut. And right now, my gut's telling me that you're my number-one suspect.'

'Cupboard!' shouted Pest. 'Let's put him in the cupboard!'

'No,' said LeCarre. 'You know why? Because there's something else I believe in. Justice. No man goes in a cupboard until he's had a chance to tell his side of the story.

I think it's time I took you in for questioning, Professor Little-Hope. Don't you?'

Little-Hope's frizzy red head of hair bobbed up and down meekly. Why? Because he was nodding. That was why.

# TWENTY

Little-Hope's fingers were shaking too much to roll the cigarette.

'Here, let me help you with that, Professor,' said LeCarre, taking the tobacco and rolling papers and assembling Little-Hope's cigarette for him like it was a toy from a Kinder Egg. LeCarre had never smoked but he was an expert at rolling cigarettes. He found the process meditative and liked the fact that he looked cool while doing it, something he'd always found difficult to achieve when constructing toys from Kinder Eggs. He'd often spend a whole evening rolling cigarettes at home and had a drawer full of unsmoked rollies. Perhaps one day he'd give them to his daughter Destiny as a gift.

LeCarre handed the now fully rolled cigarette to Little-Hope.

'Thank you. I shouldn't smoke inside, really.'

'Who's to stop you? Eli Quartz is dead. It's your house now,' said LeCarre.

'I didn't ... I promise you, I didn't have anything to do with it.'

'With what, Professor?' said LeCarre.

'The m-m-m—'

'Spit it out!'

'The murders!'

'I just had a closer look at the tusk,' said LeCarre. 'It's still there in the music room, with Quartz's blood on it. Know what I found?'

'Wh-wh-wh ...'

'What? Is that what you're trying to say? The word "what"?'

'Y-y-yes.'

'I found traces of tobacco, Professor. You think if I call up forensics, when the snow is gone, you think they'll be able to match the tobacco on the tusk with the tobacco stains on your fingers, Professor?'

'I don't know,' said Little-Hope, sweat pouring down his geeky face.

'*You don't know?* If you've never held the tusk then

your tobacco wouldn't be on it, right? There are no other smokers here.'

'I'm so confused.'

'You're supposed to be the brainbox, Professor. If you're confused, then we really are in trouble. Tell me, did you know Eli Quartz was planning on leaving his entire considerable fortune to your History department?'

'I had no idea,' said Little-Hope, now puffing on his cancerous cylinder.

'You had no idea?' said LeCarre.

'None,' said Little-Hope.

LeCarre narrowed his eyes to the size and shape of accusatory butter beans.

'I mean, he'd made some donations to the department before. I knew he cared about history.'

'He cared about history, so you made him history, is that the way it went, Professor?' said LeCarre.

'Shouldn't I have a lawyer present?' said Little-Hope.

LeCarre threw his tumbler of brandy against the wall, shattering it into roughly one hundred and twenty pieces.

'You know who ask for their lawyers, Little-Hope? Guilty men, that's who.'

'Really? Innocent men never ask for their lawyers?'

'Never!' said Detective Roger LeCarre, a man capable of

playing both good cop and bad cop, all by himself. He was the Christian Bale of policing – he had range. 'You know what the problem is with History, Professor?'

'What? What's the problem with History, Detective?'

Little-Hope seemed genuinely curious. He might have been the distinguished professor, but it was Detective Roger LeCarre who was giving the lesson. What *was* the problem with History?

'You're too greedy,' said LeCarre. 'There's always more of it. It's not like Geography. In Geography, once you've learned the capitals of the world, you're done. You've finished Geography. Nothing more to learn. In Mathematics, once you've learned all the sums, once you can count to the highest number, you're done. There's your degree. Congratulations. You're a mathematician now. I mean, thanks to calculators you're pretty pointless, but at least you can say you've completed it. Not in History. Every day there's a little bit more History to learn. Stuff keeps happening and you and your cabal want to study all of it. That kind of appetite can be expensive. Studying all that History costs money. That's why people like you have to court people like Eli Quartz. Eli Quartz was a big fish and you caught him. How did you do it, Professor? Show him a bit of ankle, did you? Offer to introduce him to Simon Schama?'

'It wasn't like that,' said Little-Hope.

'Then how was it, Professor? Tell me. I'm dying to know. Dying. Just like the two men you killed,' said LeCarre.

'I didn't kill anyone!'

'Then who killed them? It happened in the past. I thought you were an expert on the past, Professor! Shouldn't you know?' said LeCarre, making a point so smart, it felt like *he* was the one with a doctorate.

'I have no idea. I really don't.' Little-Hope looked at the floor. 'I can see how it looks, Detective.'

'How does it look, Professor? Enlighten me.'

'It looks like, well, it looks like, if all the money . . . if all of Quartz's money was going towards my History department, then . . . well, then, I had a motive for killing him.'

'You're damn well right it looks like that!' said LeCarre, pushing the sound up a decibel on the mixing desk of his own voice.

'Detective, I didn't know. I didn't know I would be . . . ' Little-Hope corrected himself, 'my department would be getting all that cash when he died. I had no idea. To be honest, wasn't he worth billions? I don't know what we'll do with it all . . . '

'Buy more books on the Nazis, I expect,' said LeCarre. 'I thought I'd read them all but it seems there's another one out every week. If you want my advice, wait until they come out in paperback. Maybe then you won't have to kill any more billionaires.'

'I didn't do it.'

If Little-Hope was lying then he was a good liar, but Devon was full of good liars. Detective Roger LeCarre knew that only too well. When he and Carrie had had their bathroom fitted, the builder had given a price that, on reflection, he must have known he'd end up overshooting. Everywhere LeCarre turned, there were liars. The books on the shelves, most of them were fiction, pure fiction, which is another word for lies.

LeCarre stood at the window and looked out over the snow-swallowed rose garden. So white. Whiter than may-pole dancing, whiter than a Glastonbury crowd.

'This isn't your first time at Powderham Castle, is it, Professor?' he said.

'No. It's not.'

'How many times have you been here, would you say?'

'I couldn't. Too many times to count, I expect. I must have been coming here for thirty years. It's a very significant part of this area's history and, well, I'm a local historian.'

'I expect you know every nook and cranny of this place, don't you, Professor? *Every* nook and cranny. Did you know the old family?'

Little-Hope swallowed.

'Yes. I did.'

'How well?'

'Not very, very, very well.'

'How many verys would you say, then? One? Two?'

'One?'

'One. So, you knew them "very well"?'

'I suppose you could say that, yes.'

'I just did,' said LeCarre, as if he'd just won some kind of competition. 'Tell me about them. The old family.'

'The Tenterhooks?' Little-Hope had the air of a man who desperately didn't want to say the wrong thing, the thing that would get him into trouble.

'Yes. The Tenterhooks. Tell me about the Tenterhooks,' said LeCarre.

Much had been said about the fact that Eli Quartz had purchased the house and the title from the previous earl. Nothing had yet been said of the man from whom he bought them.

'The Tenterhooks, well, they were the original family who built the castle, back in the fourteenth century. They made their money in the scone trade. If you ate a scone sometime before 1900, the chances were, it was a Tenterhook scone. The reason this manor house is a castle, the reason it's fortified, is because for a long time the scone business was a dangerous one. You've heard of the Scone Wars, I'm sure, Detective.'

'Of course.'

Asking a Devonian if they'd heard of the Scone Wars was like asking an Indonesian if they'd heard of Joko Widodo, who, by the way, at the time of writing is the President of Indonesia.

'Of course you have. Well, as you know, Detective, tensions about the order in which jam and cream were applied, the pronunciation of scone, or scone if you prefer, were for a long time very violent. This castle played a central role in the Scone Wars with Cornwall.'

LeCarre had recently attempted to sidestep the scone pronunciation controversy – whether to rhyme the word with cone or con – by pronouncing it 'scine'.

'So what happened?' asked LeCarre.

'It took a long time, centuries in fact, but gradually, the strength of feeling regarding scones, about the exact manner in which a cream tea should be presented, faded. Of course, it's still there.'

'You bet it is!' said LeCarre, who just last month had investigated a knife fight in Saltash, right on the Devon and Cornwall border, triggered by a disagreement about scones.

'It is. You're correct. There are still skirmishes. But the two counties are no longer at war over the matter. And that, in a strange way, was perhaps the family's downfall.'

'Elaborate,' said LeCarre, because it was what he wanted Anthony Little-Hope to do.

'People are still passionate about cream teas, Detective, but not as passionate as they once were. Other things have come into our lives. Television, the internet . . . '

'KitKat Chunkies,' said LeCarre.

'Certainly. KitKat Chunkies. People have a wide range of things to spend their hard-earned money on. When this castle was built, it was just pasties and cream teas, they were the only luxuries available to the common man. Now, the money someone might have previously spent on a cream tea could easily go on any number of other things. The Tenterhooks didn't anticipate the drop-off in scone revenue that the last fifty years or so have brought about. They didn't prepare, they didn't diversify their business into other areas like video gaming or . . . '

'KitKat Chunkies,' said LeCarre.

'Sure, KitKat Chunkies. Eventually, the financial pressure of maintaining Powderham became too much. When Eli Quartz arrived with his offer for the former earl, well, he simply couldn't say no.'

'And that turned out to be good news for Exeter University, didn't it, Professor? For its coffers.'

'Mr Quartz has been generous.'

LeCarre's gut told him to take a punt.

'I couldn't help but notice a Tesla parked here when I arrived. I had assumed it was Eli Quartz's. It's yours, isn't it, Professor?'

'Um, yes. I can't see what that has to do ...'

'Quartz's donations, they've been good for you personally, haven't they? Increased your salary?' said LeCarre.

'I suppose. Look, if you want to find a connection, I'm sure you can. It's actually a very economical vehicle,' said Little-Hope.

'You're starting to develop expensive tastes, Professor. Expensive tastes for a nerd,' said LeCarre. 'Why do you think Mr Quartz was donating all this money to your department? Why History?'

'I can't be sure, but I have a theory.'

'Go on. I'm *fascinated*.' LeCarre worried that the word 'fascinated' had come out sarcastic when he actually didn't mean it to. He was genuinely interested.

'Quartz wanted to be considered a great man, but he was a modern man from a relatively infant country. He chose to settle in Devon, in the "old world", because he didn't feel grounded. Buying a castle, financially associating himself with my History department, gave him, he thought, a chance to say, "I am a great man for the ages, my greatness spans centuries." It was all a little embarrassing, if you ask me.'

'And yet you were happy to be the beneficiary,' said LeCarre.

Little-Hope took a nervous drag on his cigarette.

'Ever heard of the Grey Lady, Professor?'

Little-Hope laughed.

'Something funny?' said LeCarre.

'Yes, I've heard of her. It is, of course, nonsense. Ghosts aren't real, Detective. You know that.'

'Do I?' said LeCarre. 'If I were you, I'm not sure I'd be so quick to eliminate other suspects.'

Little-Hope's trembling hand attempted one final puff but there was nothing there. He had smoked the entire cigarette.

'Is there anything else I can assist you with, Detective?'

'Not now, no.'

Little-Hope got up to leave.

'Oh, one more thing, Professor?'

Little-Hope rotated his academic's body, nervously. 'Yes, Detective?'

'I'm trying to remember. In the chapel, at the funeral, you were sitting next to me, weren't you?'

'Um ... ' Little-Hope's eyes went to the ceiling, in performative thought. 'Yes. Yes, I think I may have been.'

'Thank you, Professor. You've been ... ' LeCarre paused for emphasis, 'very helpful.'

# TWENTY-ONE

*Tick. Tock. Tick. Tock. Tick. Tock.*

The guests sat quietly, no playing cards in their hands. The time for games was over. They looked out over the frozen landscape as the low January sun was saying its goodbyes. That was something Eli Quartz and the Bishop of Exeter never had the chance to do – say goodbye. Not that the sun did either really, because suns don't talk, but you get the point.

Another night at Powderham, that was guaranteed. Their survival was not. There were six of them now. Six little piggies, ready for the slaughter.

Professor Anthony Little-Hope was rattled, rattled like a baby's toy, rattled like a rattle. He'd get up, he'd sit down, he'd walk over to the window and stare. What was he looking for? Redemption? A way out? He didn't look like a murderer, but then, what did a murderer look like? LeCarre had seen all types, all shapes and sizes in his time. He didn't fancy Little-Hope's chances in prison. LeCarre had found it hard enough in the cupboard, and he was as tough as they came. A man like Anthony Little-Hope? Prison would chew him up but never spit him out, just digest him, like a bar of chocolate – *a bar of chocolate that had murdered two people.*

Cynthia Pest had taken to reading a book. Or at least doing an impression of someone who was. Her eyes never seemed to be on the page. Instead, they darted nervously around the room. Was she looking to see what the murderer might do next? Or was she looking for her next victim? Cynthia had the air of a former *Blue Peter* presenter who'd fallen on hard times. You could see that, as a younger woman, she'd have had a sort of spunky charm. The world she was born into had never required her to work, supposed LeCarre. So she'd devoted her energies to partying, and that had been her undoing. If her habits didn't shorten her life, she still had another forty, fifty years ahead of her, but it was hard to imagine what she might do with them. Maybe this weekend of enforced quiet would be good for her.

LeCarre could see the appeal of a life that revolved around partying, around the night-time. A life that never saw breakfast television sober. His drug of choice was booze and he liked it a lot. Too much? Carrie thought so. But then Carrie thought that AJ Odudu was going to win series nineteen of *Strictly Come Dancing* and she'd been proven wrong on that. What Carrie didn't understand was that Roger LeCarre was a cop, and cops needed something to turn to when things got dark. If you saw the things LeCarre saw – murder, robbery, people entering the yellow box at a junction when their exit road wasn't clear – you needed a drink from time to time. Also, alcohol wasn't illegal, so what was the problem?

Angela Peacock sat still and did nothing, as if she were posing for a portrait. Any painter who managed to repli- cate her beauty would be a very good painter indeed. Was LeCarre allowing her appearance to project onto her an innocence she didn't possess? Possibly. All shapes and sizes. But he'd never seen a murderer like this. To be murdered by Angela Peacock could almost be considered a privilege.

Thanks to the fact he had a wife and daughter, Roger LeCarre respected women and could never see them as mere objects. There was so much more to them than met the eye. One week, for example, they'd had a woman on their pub quiz team and she'd been excellent, particularly on TV and celebrity stuff. And yet, if LeCarre could have Angela

Peacock encased in glass and transported to his house, he'd pay whatever it took to make it happen. Sure, legally he might run into trouble and Carrie would almost certainly have a problem with it, especially if he put the glass-encased Angela in his preferred position at the foot of their bed, but you couldn't put a price on art and Angela Peacock was, most definitely, a work of art. And a good one too. Not one of those weird ones that won the Turner Prize. LeCarre despaired at that sort of rubbish. One of these days I'm just going to do a turd, drive it up to London, enter it for the Turner Prize and become a millionaire, thought LeCarre, satirically.

LeCarre had to consider the fact that Angela could have committed the murders. No one knew the castle better than her and her father. He couldn't let her beauty blind him. Her stillness was cold. A cold-hearted killer? Maybe.

Arthur Peacock stood by the marble fireplace, not far from where Eli Quartz had died less than twenty-four hours before, watching everyone. Everyone was watching everyone. Six people, twelve eyes, all trained on each other. All moving around, pointing in different directions. It was a bit odd, actually.

Arthur Peacock was back to his rigid self, but behind closed doors LeCarre had seen a softer side. Tragedy had struck the Peacocks and Arthur was feeling the pain. The Grey Lady? LeCarre was reluctant to discount it as a possibility. A murdering ghost made about as much sense as anything else in this goddamn case. One thing was for sure: Chief Superintendent Beverley Chang wouldn't be happy if LeCarre suggested she call up the CPS to ask them if they could charge a six-hundred-year-old vision. LeCarre chuckled at the thought.

Patricia Beresford, who'd started to knit, looked at him, her elbows bouncing up and down, like she was greedily digging into a meal, something her frame suggested wasn't an irregular occurrence. From prime suspect to bottom of the pile, her near-death experience had taken the heat off Patricia Beresford. You don't kill two people then poison yourself. Not unless you were faking it – but faking it just so happened to be what Patricia Beresford did for a living.

'Excuse me, where are you going?' said Beresford.

Cynthia Pest was heading out of the room.

'To the bathroom. Is that a crime?' said Pest.

'No. It's just, under the circumstances, shouldn't we all be ... monitored?' said Beresford.

'You're welcome to watch me if you like, Ms Beresford,' said Pest.

'Oh, don't be so revolting,' said Beresford.

'Well, that's what you're suggesting, isn't it?' said Pest.

'What do you think, Detective?' said Beresford. 'Surely people can't just come and go as they please. Under the circumstances.'

'I think people need to be allowed to carry out their natural . . . ' LeCarre, conscious that he was in refined company, searched for a classy word for a piss. 'Obligations. Just don't take too long please, Ms Pest.'

'Certainly not,' said Pest, sarcastically. 'I wouldn't want to miss out on all this terrific fun we're having.'

As Cynthia Pest exited, LeCarre took in the room and tried to see it as it had been the night before, at the moment of Eli Quartz's murder. He had been standing in front of the fireplace, holding one end of the tusk, Eli Quartz holding the other. The Peacocks, as he remembered it, had stood at the edge of the room, one by each entrance. The guests – Pest, Beresford, Little-Hope and the Bishop of Exeter – had stood near to where the action was taking place.

LeCarre closed his eyes and tried to see it as a photograph. Had he known, at the time, that a murder was about to take place, he'd have pressed the clicker on his photographic memory. Always be on the lookout for clues. Murder can strike at any time. Especially in Exeter, the murder capital of East Devon. But he wasn't in Exeter, he was in Powderham

Castle. It wasn't supposed to be like this. LeCarre had always thought that he followed crime but perhaps it was the other way around and crime followed him wherever he went. Maybe he should run away to the Sahara, leave crime there and return to a crime-free Britain. No. Crime was smarter than that. You couldn't trick it, you had to confront it – face to face.

LeCarre's eyes were still closed. A picture began to form of the moment before Quartz's murder. Beresford was beside the piano, closer to Quartz. Then, going left along the line, came the Bishop, then Pest, then Little-Hope, closest to LeCarre. All were close to the action. All within striking distance. What they had done was still a mystery.

And the thunderbolt? The sudden darkness? That had been real. How could any of them have known that that was about to happen, at that exact moment? A spontaneous murder? An opportunity taken, in the blackout? Or something planned? Perhaps the Bishop had arranged the thunderbolt with God. But the Bishop was dead now. Did he kill Quartz and then someone else took revenge on him? Too many questions, not enough answers. A very bad pub quiz round indeed.

'How long has the Duchess been gone now?' said Little-Hope.

'Too long,' said Beresford. 'She's up to something. I know

bad eggs when I see them and that girl is the baddest egg in the box.'

'This is ridiculous,' said Little-Hope. 'This situation is unsustainable. We can't just wait another night. We're sitting ducks! We'll all be dead by dawn.'

'Oh, don't be so hysterical,' said Beresford. 'If you'd done as much repertory theatre as I have, then you'd learn that all this fussing does you no good.'

'The Belvedere Tower,' said Little-Hope. 'Mr Peacock. How far is it? What if I were to make my way down there and ring the bell? Then we could get some help. Surely, if Detective LeCarre's colleagues knew the situation we're in, they'd have the equipment to get to us. Get us out of here, before it's too late?'

'I think it's best we all stay together,' said LeCarre.

'Well, where is Ms Pest, then?' said Little-Hope. 'She's been gone ten minutes.'

A number two, thought LeCarre, using his deductive mind.

'It's too treacherous,' said Arthur Peacock. 'It must be nearly a mile to the Belvedere. Down a dirt track. It's starting to get dark. There's are no lights out there. You'll freeze to death before you get to the tower and even if you did, I'm not sure that the bell works any more, anyway. It would be very foolish, sir.'

'So we're just going to wait here?' said Little-Hope, before his mind turned back to Cynthia Pest. *'Where is she?'*

'I can go and check on her?' said Angela Peacock.

'No,' said LeCarre. 'I think it's best if I do. I'm the professional here, after all.'

'The professional who let two men die on his watch,' said Beresford. The words stung, especially coming, as they did, from the county's Queen Bee. LeCarre caught one of Angela's stunning eyes; it seemed to offer sympathy.

'I won't be long,' he said, as he left the room and went looking for Cynthia Pest. What he found would change *everything*. At least regards to the situation at Powderham Castle, anyway.

# TWENTY-TWO

Sex. He recognised the sound the second he heard it, coming from the servants' quarters. Sex. Vigorous, rhythmic, West Country sex. Two bodies making percussive love against the furniture. Two voices moaning in delight. Sex featuring two participants. *Two participants.*

Only Cynthia Pest had left the room.

Detective Roger LeCarre had always been a keen enthusiast for sex, ever since he'd first heard about it, in biology class at Totnes Grammar School for Boys at the age of fifteen. The teacher had asked the pupils to turn their textbooks to page 52 and as the rest of the class let out squeamish yelps at the graphic, scientific diagrams, LeCarre had thought to himself, That . . . that looks like something worth pursuing. And he had. With diligent gusto.

Just nine years later, when he'd first been able to put his theories into practice, when he'd first managed to find a partner willing to join him in the penetrative pleasures he so desired, it had been everything he had hoped for. And more. And do you know what? He was good at it. *Real* good. Better than any man in the county. At least that's what some of the women had told him, under heavy questioning. Detective Roger LeCarre's body was his instrument and he was its virtuoso player. It was as if Yo-Yo Ma were to one day become so at one with his cello that he *became* his cello. A walking cello man, having sex with beautiful women.

LeCarre approached sex like a vital food group, some-thing that he needed to digest as often as possible. Fibre, carbohydrates, fat, protein, alcohol and sex. Had his appe-tites put strains on his marriage? Yes. Had he and Carrie come to an unsaid agreement that allowed him to satisfy those appetites? Yes. Was Carrie aware of the parameters of that unsaid agreement? Probably not.

The fact was, when it came to sex, Detective Roger LeCarre was a world-class athlete. It would be a disservice to the sport if he were to restrict his activities to just one partner. This year was going to be different, though. He had made a solemn, monk-like vow to himself to have sex with no more than ten women – less than one a month. It was a mark of his deep and unwavering love for Carrie LeCarre. He was now a world-class athlete who didn't play the tour, only the odd exhibition match.

The servants' quarters were through the dining room, along a small passageway and down a humble flight of stairs. A departure from the grandeur of the rest of the house. LeCarre approached slowly, like he was performing a drugs bust, but he wasn't. This was a sex bust. The question dominating his mind was – who was having sex with Cynthia Pest? Who was making her moan in regal ecstasy?

The Grey Lady? She was the only rational explanation – the only unaccounted-for person at Powderham Castle. The rest, everyone but for Roger LeCarre and Cynthia Pest, were in the music room where he had left them.

In all his years of experience, all his erotic exploits, LeCarre had never made love to a ghost. Frankly, until this point it hadn't even occurred to him that it was a possibility. On a purely practical level, LeCarre assumed it would be too difficult to get any kind of purchase on such a wispy figure. This was a weekend for surprises. An invite to a party at what turned out to be a snowed-in castle, framed for two murders, and now this – a ghost having sex with a Duchess. He certainly had some stories to tell next time he was at the Crown and Goose.

*If there was a next time.*

LeCarre was now at the bottom of the stairs. A step more, a turn to the right, and he'd be looking at the copulating couple. What was the etiquette? Walking in on people having sex – that was rude. His parents had taught him that. But this situation was different. There was a murderer at large and the medium of erotic sound suggested there was a new suspect on the premises.

Cynthia saw LeCarre before LeCarre was able to compute the scene before him.

'Uh ... Detective ... '

Pest's face gleamed with mid-coital lust. She was still in her polka-dot dress, her hands flat down on the servants' dining table. Behind her stood, not a ghost, but a man, a man LeCarre had never seen before, pulling up his muddy trousers.

LeCarre asked the question. The only question that seemed appropriate under the circumstances. The question that simply had to be asked.

'Who the fuck are you?'

'This is Seth, Detective,' said Cynthia Pest. 'Seth Tuckerton.'

'You're a copper, is it?' he said.

Seth's voice was gravelly, of the earth. It sounded local,

agricultural, ancient. A bit like the comedian, Jethro, the one who was on *The Generation Game* sometimes in the 90s.

Determining Seth's age was difficult. He looked like a man who'd spent little time indoors, so weatherbeaten was his face. Red and dry and fortified by rum and pasties. The top of his head bore messy, thinning black hair. On his cheeks were confident lamb chop sideburns. His brown eyes sparkled with Devon mischief. His nose was the size and shape of an upside-down travel-size tube of toothpaste. Below his big, chapped lips was a strong, stubbled chin. If Seth had never pushed a plough, then his body suggested that the generations that came before him had certainly passed down their plough-pushing genes. Big arms, like full laundry bags. A hairy, sweating, muscular chest. His penis, thankfully, was no longer in sight and was safely deposited inside his trousers. Detective Roger LeCarre was heterosexual, so heterosexual in fact that he was proud to say that he'd never seen another man's genital length. He had no intention of changing that now.

'I thought . . . '

'We were the only ones here?' said Pest.

'Yes,' said LeCarre.

'Seth's been at Powderham since he was a little boy,' said Pest.

Seth lit himself a cigarette and offered the pack to Cynthia and LeCarre, who both declined.

'You've got some explaining to do, Cynthia,' said LeCarre.

Pest swallowed. She most certainly did.

# TWENTY-THREE

LeCarre felt seasick. This case had nothing to cling on to. Just wave after wave of new, confusing information. Like an episode of some cerebral Netflix drama. LeCarre was in choppy waters and he didn't have a life jacket. Anything could happen next. It was sink or swim.

They – LeCarre, Pest, Seth – were all standing in the servants' dining room. The smell of sex still hung in the air like an erotically scented drone.

'Is sex a crime now, Detective?' Pest provocatively posited. 'I do hope not. I think I may be a multiple offender.'

'Sex is no crime but harbouring a murderer is,' said LeCarre.

'Seth? A murderer! Seth's just a big teddy bear, aren't you, darling?' said Pest.

'What you need to understand, Seth, is that this ain't no teddy bears' picnic. Two people have died. There are things I need to know. Who are you and how did you get here?' said LeCarre, subconsciously widening his stance in case violence arrived. If Seth was a teddy bear, he'd been working out at some kind of teddy bear gymnasium.

'Seth is—'

LeCarre interrupted Pest.

'I'd like the man to speak for himself, please.'

Seth spoke with the humble simplicity of a man of the soil. If black tie events weren't Roger LeCarre's scene then they most certainly weren't Seth's. He looked like a man who'd never stepped inside a Waitrose, let alone an earl's manor house.

'Powderham's my home, sir.'

'Then where have you been?' said LeCarre. 'We've been here all weekend. Where have you been?'

'Oh, I don't live in the castle, sir. There's an outhouse, just over there . . . ' Seth gestured behind him.

Seth didn't look like he'd been waist deep in the snow. He caught LeCarre looking at his legs and pointed to the ground.

'Trap door. It's a bit of a squeeze but there's a passageway between here and there. Few more pasties and I won't be able to do it any more.'

'You live in the outhouse, do you?' asked LeCarre.

'Mr Tenterhook used to let me stay there. On account of all the gardening and whatnot I did for him.'

'I see,' said LeCarre. 'And Mr Quartz?'

'Oh ... he ... ' Seth looked down.

'Mr Quartz let you do the same, didn't he, Seth?' said Cynthia Pest.

'Yeah. Yeah, Mr Quartz let me do the same, yeah,' said Seth. LeCarre used his detective skills to detect that Pest was leading Seth into an answer that hid a truth. Whatever arrangement Seth had had with the previous earl didn't seem to be as much of a comfortable arrangement with Mr Quartz.

'And what did you do for Mr Tenterhook? And Mr Quartz? What do you do here at Powderham and why the crap didn't I know you were here?'

'Like I said, gardening and whatnot,' said Seth. 'There's always something that needs doing. Tending to the guttering, fixing doors and that. There'll be lots to do after this weekend, that's for sure. What with all the snow and all. The grounds will be a mess.'

'And what's this?' said LeCarre, pointing between the two of them. 'This relationship. Seth your bit of rough, is he, Ms Pest?'

'That's none of your business, Detective,' said Pest, her lips hinting at a smirk. LeCarre had always heard of the penchant aristocratic women had for gardeners. 'If you must know, I've known Seth since we were teenagers. I used to come here and play with the Tenterhook children. Seth was a boy then too. My mama and papa wanted me to mix with the Tenterhook boys. I think they hoped I might marry one of them and create some kind of Devon dynasty. It was Seth I had a soft spot for. We've always had a little thing for each other. What you witnessed just then – well, will you think less of me, Detective, if I tell you it wasn't the first time Seth has bent me over at Powderham?'

The others would be wondering where they were. Heck, the others might be killing each other right now. Much as he'd like to, now wasn't the time to run through the sexual history of the Duchess of Totnes. But there were still some questions sitting on Detective Roger LeCarre's inquisitive lips and they needed to be asked.

'Ms Pest . . . '

'Yes, Detective.'

'Did you know that Seth was here all along?'

'What do you mean?' said Pest.

'You know damn well what I mean, Duchess,' said LeCarre. 'We've been here for nearly twenty-four hours

195

now. Two people have died. A murderer is on the grounds. Did you know that there was another person here at Powderham all along?'

Pest laughed nervously, but it wasn't yet 6.30 and they weren't listening to BBC Radio 4. It wasn't the time for laughing.

'I suppose I knew Seth could well be here,' said Pest.

'And you didn't think to mention it?' said LeCarre.

'I wasn't sure. I haven't been here for a couple of years. Not since Mr Quartz took over. I didn't know if Seth was still living here.'

'But you went looking for him,' said LeCarre.

'I felt like I needed a friend.'

This was no ordinary friendship. LeCarre had friends. He played squash with them. He went for a pint with them. He didn't let them bend him over tables.

'How did you contact him? There's no signal.'

Pest pointed to a landline phone. *A landline phone.* In a six-hundred-year-old castle, it somehow felt like the most antiquated thing there.

'There's a direct line between here and the outhouse,' said Pest. 'I remembered from when I was a child.' Pest looked up, coyly. 'I was lonely.'

'All right, well, you're not going anywhere now, Seth.

You're staying in the castle. I need to know where every-one is at all times. If we're going to stay alive, then that's essential.'

Just then, Angela Peacock's stunning feet ran frantically down the stairs and into the servants' dining room. She looked like a woman delivering news, but first she was a woman delivering shock. Shock at the sight of Seth.

'Seth!' she said. 'You're not supposed to ...'

'Sorry, Angela,' said Seth. 'The Duchess, she called for me ...'

'I suppose you can stay inside. If my father allows it.' Angela Peacock took a deep breath and turned to LeCarre. 'Detective, there's something you need to know.'

'Yes?' said LeCarre.

'Professor Little-Hope.'

'Yes?'

'He's gone.'

# TWENTY-FOUR

The number of people hadn't changed. Just as Seth had arrived, Anthony Little-Hope had left. One in, one out. Powderham Castle was operating the same policy as Exeter's Fever nightclub on a busy Friday night.

The story of Little-Hope's departure was told to LeCarre.

'There was no persuading him,' said Arthur Peacock. 'I told him . . . it's not safe out there. But he insisted on leaving. Said he was going to the Belvedere Tower to ring the bell and get us help. Of course, I haven't heard a sound.'

'His eyes!' said Patricia Beresford. 'His eyes were guilty as hell. He knew that once the police got here, there was no escape.'

They were sitting in the music room again but no music was to be heard. No real music. Only the music of misery, the music of murder. Why did people keep saying 'once the police get here'? LeCarre was still in his tux. Strip him of his usual outfit – his leather jacket, his brown brogues – did people just see him as another civilian? LeCarre had always thought that his status and rank were there for all to see at all times – in his posture, in his rugged eyes. Maybe he'd lost something this weekend. Maybe he was just the same as the rest of them. Another chump stuck in a castle, at the mercy of a murderer, terrified of being next. Maybe he was only alive as long as the murderer *let him* be alive.

Detective Roger LeCarre was a man used to being in charge of his own destiny. Sure, he had responsibilities: to his family, to the Devon and Cornwall police force, to his pub quiz team. He took those responsibilities seriously, but the point was that he *chose* those responsibilities. He could leave them any time he liked. Fly to Costa Rica and become a surfing instructor. Cash in his savings and open up a Subway franchise in Plympton. Take up the saxophone and record a Grammy-winning jazz album. All these options were open to him, there for him to take up, any time he liked. He didn't do them, not because he couldn't but because he didn't want to.

Now, all choices were closed off to him. He wasn't, really, even a police officer any more. If the others suspected him again, they could throw him back in the cupboard and there'd be nothing he could do about it. He was a man, stuck with unfamiliar people in an unfamiliar place, imprisoned by the cruelty of weather. It was easy to see why Anthony Little-Hope had left.

With the arrival of Seth, a new dynamic had surfaced. Seth, the Peacocks and Pest had history. With Pest a long-time regular visitor to Powderham and the Peacocks and Seth being long-time residents, LeCarre and Patricia Beresford were now in a minority. They were the outsiders. That was fine by LeCarre. He'd been an outsider all his goddamn life.

Beresford hadn't been able to bring herself to look at Seth. The arrival of a new man was terrifying, especially one with biceps the size of his. The first thing LeCarre had done was assess his height – the same as Cynthia Pest's, the same as the murderer, the same as the others – five feet eight inches. What were the odds? If someone wrote it, you'd never believe it.

Seth was as much of a suspect as anyone else. Maybe more so. He knew the castle, probably knew every trap door, every secret passageway – of which there were a surprising number. The fact he hadn't made himself known was suspicious too. It was hard to imagine someone being in an outhouse, just a few yards from Patricia Beresford, the county's most legendary radio actress, and not wanting to come by and meet her. That kind of opportunity only came once in a lifetime. Perhaps he didn't even know she was there. It wasn't clear how his relationship with Eli Quartz was. Perhaps he hadn't even been made aware of the occasion.

'Tell me exactly what happened with Little-Hope,' said LeCarre. 'How did he leave?'

'Ms Beresford – I hope I'm not being impolite here – Ms Beresford went to the restroom,' said Arthur Peacock. 'Little-Hope started yelling about how we were all doomed, about how he was going to get help. I told him not to go. You city people, you don't understand. Nature is cruel. It's two miles to the nearest supermarket here. We're as isolated as it's possible to be. In this weather, I'd be surprised if he lasted twenty minutes before he froze to death. All he had was a simple overcoat. A pair of shoes. He wasn't equipped for that kind of terrain.'

It was dark outside now. They'd heard no bell coming from the tower. Could Little-Hope really be dead? Perhaps he'd just gone to prepare for his next murder. Perhaps he'd return with a rescue party.

'Shouldn't some of us go search for him, like?' said Seth, using the word 'like' unnecessarily, in the way that teenagers, Geordies and the uneducated tend to do.

'We'd be walking to our deaths,' said Arthur Peacock.

'Detective?' said Pest, turning to LeCarre.

'I think the safest thing is for us to stay together,' said LeCarre. 'We'll stay down here, in the music room, for the evening. Peacock, do all the bedrooms have locks on the doors?'

'Yes, Detective. I fitted them myself.'

'Then presumably you have a key that opens them all?' said LeCarre, furrowing his handsome brow.

'That I do. I can put that key somewhere safe, if it would make everybody feel more comfortable.'

'Who's to say he doesn't have another?' said Patricia Beresford, correctly identifying the problem. All pretence of trust had evaporated. Everyone suspected everyone. It reminded LeCarre of pub quizzing in the early days of smart phones. Every team thought every other team was cheating. LeCarre had called the council to see if they could turn off the internet between the hours of 8 p.m. and 10 p.m. on Monday nights, when the Crown and Goose pub quiz ran. Too much red tape, they'd said. No wonder they never got anything done. No wonder the roads were covered with potholes. They couldn't even do something simple like turning the internet off once a week for a couple of hours so that a pub quiz could run fairly.

'All the doors have bolts too,' said Angela Peacock. 'You can't open a bolt from the outside.'

'You can kick it open, surely?' said Beresford.

'At least that would make a loud sound,' said LeCarre. 'The murderer needs to know that if they break into someone's room, then the rest of us will hear it. This is the best we can do. We'll all stay down here for the next few hours. Have a pleasant evening together. As pleasant as we can under the circumstances. Then we'll lock ourselves into our rooms. If nobody does anything stupid, that should see us through until morning. Then the weather will clear, I'm sure, and we can find our way out of here.'

LeCarre looked at each of his castle companions.

'It's as good a plan as any,' said Pest.

'Ms Beresford?' said LeCarre.

'It's Saturday night! I have a standing reservation at Café Rouge on Saturday nights. They'll be wondering where I am.'

'There's nothing we can do about that, Ms Beresford. Control what you can control,' said LeCarre. 'The plan as I stated it. For lack of a better option, are you on board with it, Ms Beresford?'

Patricia Beresford nodded her locally famous head.

'Seth?'

'A night inside the big house!' said Seth. 'It'll be an honour.'

'Mr Peacock?'

'Yes, Detective.'

LeCarre turned to Angela Peacock, who looked at him in admiration. Detective Roger LeCarre had a way of making women feel safe. In another life he could have made a good bungee-jump operator.

'Thank you, Detective,' she said. 'For everything you're doing for us.'

'It's my job,' said LeCarre.

'Well, you're going above and beyond. We have plenty of supplies. If you give us an hour, myself and my father can serve you all a meal.'

'Wait, wait. No, absolutely not!' said Patricia Beresford. 'If you'll remember, somebody has already attempted to poison me. I'm not taking that risk. Absolutely not!'

The room paused. Patricia Beresford had a point. What was the sense of arranging to lock yourself in your room, only to hand your digestive system over to the potential murderer?

'Pizza?' said Seth. 'There's a Papa Johns in Exminster that delivers out here.'

'Do they do moules marinière?' said Beresford. 'On

Saturday nights, I always have moules marinière at Café Rouge.'

'Just pizza, I think,' said Seth. 'Bloody tasty, though.'

'Papa Johns will have to do,' said LeCarre.

Many years later, LeCarre realised that that was the second he should have realised that something was wrong. If they were snowed in at the castle, then how would a pizza delivery be able to get to them? The fact was that in that moment he was too immersed in the case to be able to see it properly. Roger LeCarre was the best detective in the West Country, probably the best in England, but even he didn't have the kind of brain required to notice something like that, like the discrepancy of a moped being able to get to the castle with six warm pizzas, but them not being able to escape.

The grandfather clock chimed. Seven o'clock.

'What we gonna do with the evening, then?' said Seth. 'Might as well have some fun.'

'We're going to have a party,' said Cynthia Pest. 'We simply must. I insist on it. It's Saturday night! Let's make the most of it.'

# TWENTY-FIVE

Of all of Eli Quartz's creations, that party was probably the greatest. And he didn't even get to see it. Once, when Carrie had taken Destiny to visit her mother, Roger had found himself in the house on his own. Forced to feed himself, LeCarre decided to put together a meal with what little ingredients were left in the kitchen: a tub of Philadelphia, a leek, one packet of icing sugar and a jar of rogan josh paste. To his own surprise, what LeCarre made that night was the finest meal he had ever tasted. So good was it, that he ate that exact dish every night for the next two years. Things that don't seem as if they should go together just work sometimes. Well, that was that party. Six people, one of them a murderer, the rest potential victims, all of them having the night of their lives.

*At least, they were to begin with.*

Perhaps it was the threat of imminent death that allowed people to enjoy themselves. LeCarre had seen it before. No man traversed the wildly differing worlds that Devon and Cornwall offered like Detective Roger LeCarre. He'd seen the bright lights of Exeter, and its darkest corners too. He'd mixed with them all. From the lowliest hobo to the CEO of Ginsters. In the Devon ghettos, where death could strike at any time, people learned to enjoy each and every day because it might be their last. It was in the higher climes, that was where the tension was. If you ran Ginsters, you spent your days thinking about holding on to what you had, worrying about Greggs making strides into the service station sector, and never for a moment sitting back with a chicken and mushroom slice and thinking about how far you'd come.

Here – that night in Powderham Castle – they were all equal. What they had in their bank accounts didn't matter. Perhaps Marxism *could* work after all. Although, and this has to be said, if a political system requires you to engineer a scenario in which people are trapped together in castles with murderers in order to work, then it is a bad political system.

For LeCarre, what made the evening so beautiful was that he had his identity back. Earlier on that day he'd lost it, somewhere in that cupboard. But as the plan for the night was made, he felt everyone look to him to ensure their safety. He was a copper again. *In Auxilium Omnium.* That was the Devon and Cornwall Police motto. In another language for some stupid reason. Probably French. Probably at the request of some faceless Brussels bureaucrat. What did it mean? To the assistance of everybody. LeCarre had always hated it because, to him, it didn't make sense. Sure, LeCarre was ready to jump to the assistance of law-abiding citizens – old ladies crossing the road, tourists in need of directions, people who'd just been burgled – but to the assistance of *everybody*? Really? The motto seemed to imply that he should assist criminals in their crimes, give way to ram raiders, open the door for shoplifters. That night, he finally got it. 'To the assistance of everybody' meant it was his duty to do his best to keep everyone safe and when the time came, when he'd identified the perpetrator, when he had the murderer in his sights, would he assist them too? Sure. He'd assist them . . . *to jail.*

First, before the party really kicked off, came the pizzas. All those years ago, when little Roger LeCarre had taken his bedtime bath to the sound of Thelma Bertwhistle on *Jam on Top*, he could never have imagined that he would one day share a BBQ Chicken Classic with the vector of her voice,

Patricia Beresford. He allowed himself a moment to savour the occasion. Then, jolting himself back into police mode, he neatly pocketed the little plastic table in the centre of the pizza in case he needed to jab it into someone's eyes in self-defence later on in the evening.

It was Patricia Beresford who began the evening's festivities by sitting at the grand piano and treating them to a selection of Devon standards: 'Pickled in Paignton', 'I Lost my Love to Ilfracombe', 'Don't Be Leading Me Down the Tamar'. Everyone knew the words and before long, it was a singalong. By the time they got to the classic protest song 'Fuck the Cornish', the group were linking arms and swaying in tipsy unison. No matter their background, their status, they were united by one thing – a belief in their county. One of them was a killer but they were a killer *from Devon*. They all had more in common with that killer than any random person from Dorset. They all, each of them, knew that Devon had a surface area of 2,950 square miles. They knew that it had an annual total economic output of over £26 billion. They knew that it was the only county in England to have two coastlines, that the South West Coast Path ran the entire length of both, and that around 65 per cent of that coast was designated Heritage Coast. They knew that Devon County Council had sixty-two councillors and that the county was represented in the House of Commons by twelve Members of Parliament. They knew these things, not because they had spent ten minutes on the Wikipedia page for Devon and collated a series of facts to pad out a novel, but because they were all true Devonians and they were *proud* of it.

In a strange way, the group seemed to be celebrating. Two people were dead, Professor Anthony Little-Hope was missing, and yet here they were singing. They were celebrating being alive. They were the survivors. It was their duty to those who'd perished to enjoy every moment.

Cynthia Pest had discovered an old drinks cabinet, hidden in the wall, and the group had treated themselves to generous servings of brandy and lovage. The stash of the old West Country cordial, lovage, had clearly belonged to the old owners, the Tenterhooks. With the bottles unopened, the group could watch their uncorking and pour their own drinks, safe in the knowledge that poisoning was impossible. For LeCarre, brandy and lovage brought back memories of nights out as a Totnes teenager, learning how to drink in the town's ancient pubs. The drink was sweet yet punchy, like a toddler with a sugar rush.

For coppers like LeCarre, true coppers, stubbled coppers who didn't play by the rules, drink wasn't a choice but a necessity. It went with the job as much as warrant cards, truncheons and failing marriages. LeCarre let the liquor trickle down his throat, like high-octane super unleaded petrol into his Kia Ceed. This was his fuel. He'd tried to give up drink once. Bad month. Crime in Devon and Cornwall went up by 8 per cent. Detective Roger LeCarre needed alcohol to do his job, like a surveyor needed a theodolite – which, by the way, is the measuring instrument you see them looking through on the street sometimes.

Seth Tuckerton seemed excited by his rare foray into the castle's interior. His expansive agricultural face maintained a constant beaming smile. If the Peacocks were uncomfortable with his muddy boots on the antique Georgian rugs, then they didn't show it. Both the Peacocks and Tuckerton were servants, but there was a clear difference. The Peacocks were the house's public face. Any visitors were looked after by them – hence their proper, upright demeanour. Tuckerton was the house's engine room, the swan's legs, unseen by all. Not pretty, but vital to the running of the castle.

LeCarre sidled beside him and made conversation.

'I take it you've heard about the sad demise of Mr Quartz?'

'Oh yes,' said Tuckerton, his smile still remaining. 'Terrible business.'

'You don't, and I hope you don't mind me saying this, seem particularly upset,' said LeCarre.

'Any death is sad, sir,' said Tuckerton.

'Seth, would you say you had a good relationship with Mr Quartz?' asked LeCarre.

'No, sir. I hated the bastard.'

Seth Tuckerton's honesty was as refreshing as the pint of ale LeCarre hoped to be drinking in the Crown and Goose when this was all over. Usually, every suspect proclaimed their undying love and respect for the victim. Tuckerton could at least admit the truth.

'Why was that, Seth?'

'You knew where you were with the Tenterhooks,' said Tuckerton. 'Yeah, they were snooty and whatnot but I had my jobs, around the grounds and that, and they let me get on with them. Every Christmas Day, the Countess, she'd bring some Christmas pudding out for me, out in the outhouse. I loved her for it. She didn't have to do that.'

'I take it Mr Quartz didn't do the same?'

Tuckerton laughed.

'The arrangement you had with the Tenterhooks,' said LeCarre. 'You living here on the grounds and doing odd jobs for them. That still continued with Mr Quartz, though, am I right?'

'Not for much longer,' said Tuckerton. 'The bastard sent a letter through my door on New Year's Day. Didn't even say it to my face. Said they was "restructuring". Said my work was gonna be "automated" or something. There was no longer a need for a "full-time on-site groundsman". Said I had fourteen days to leave the premises. Five hundred years my family's worked on this estate and I get fourteen days to pack up and leave?'

LeCarre drained the last of his brandy and lovage.

'Sounds like you had good reason to want him dead, Seth.'

Tuckerton pushed LeCarre against the teal wall and bore his eyes into him.

'This is the problem with you city folk. You're all in a rush. You spend five minutes with a man and you think you know everything about him. I'm glad Eli Quartz is dead. But I didn't kill him.'

Detective Roger LeCarre had a rule. If you pushed Detective Roger LeCarre up against a wall then, pretty soon, you'd get pushed up against a wall yourself and Detective Roger LeCarre would be the one doing the pushing. He grabbed Tuckerton by the shirt, spun him and imposed himself.

'Maybe you did kill Eli Quartz, maybe you didn't, but what you *did* do just now is disrespect Detective Roger LeCarre. Bad move, Seth. Bad move. I'm not city folk. I'm not country folk. I'm copper folk, and copper folk don't like getting pushed up against walls. Are we clear?'

Seth swallowed. He'd done the one thing you didn't want to do in Devon and Cornwall. He'd underestimated Roger LeCarre.

'Clear,' said Tuckerton.

'Good,' said LeCarre, releasing Tuckerton from his grip. 'No hard feelings. Can I get you another brandy and lovage?'

Tuckerton nodded.

'Sure.'

'Excellent,' said LeCarre, heading back towards the drinks, endorphins surging into his body. He'd just taken a little bit of the Exeter street to Powderham Castle and it felt good. The only thing tainting the moment for him, ever so slightly, was a fear that the phrase 'copper folk' may have sounded a bit like he meant 'metal people' when he, in fact, meant police.

# TWENTY-SIX

With many more brandy and lovages consumed, the room was sufficiently lubricated and everybody appeared to be enjoying themselves. A collection of board games had been found. They started with Trivial Pursuit, with Detective Roger LeCarre the comfortable winner. Arthur Peacock won Monopoly, but LeCarre spent a good twenty minutes explaining to the group that where Trivial Pursuit was a game of skill, Monopoly was primarily a game of luck.

Then, without really thinking about what she was doing, Patricia Beresford pulled Cluedo from the pile.

'Oh, Cluedo! I love a good game of Cluedo!'

Beresford paused. They all did.

Films, books – they were all used to those reflecting their lived experience. It was not often that one could say that the piece of art that best represented what you were going through was a board game.

'I'm bored with board games,' said Cynthia Pest, using both spellings of the word in quick succession. 'I want to dance!'

The Duchess of Totnes had relaxed immeasurably since Seth Tuckerton had arrived. Every now and then they'd discreetly hold hands or steal a kiss. LeCarre caught Beresford giving a disapproving look. Perhaps she thought the classes shouldn't mix. But her mood remained jovial.

'I could play a little honky-tonk piano, if you like,' said Beresford. 'A little ragtime?'

'I was thinking more along the lines of ...' Pest turned to Tuckerton, who in turn, turned to Angela Peacock.

'I suppose we could,' said Angela.

'What?' said Pest.

'Oh, come on, we've got to,' said Tuckerton.

'*What?*' said Pest.

'The minstrels' gallery,' said Angela.

'Minstrels' gallery?' said LeCarre.

'It's a balcony in the state dining room,' said Arthur Peacock. 'Built in the sixteenth century, I think. Musicians used to perform from there on special occasions.'

'Didn't ...?' said Tuckerton.

'Yes,' said Angela Peacock.

'What?' said Pest, brimming with energy.

'Mr Quartz installed some turntables up there. And a sound system,' said Angela.

Cynthia Pest squealed with excitement.

'Oh, we have to! We have to!'

'It's getting a little late,' said Arthur Peacock. 'Shouldn't we all be going to bed at the same time? You know, for safety.'

'Well, I'm not tired,' said Patricia Beresford. 'I am an actress, after all. I come alive at night!' She winked at Seth.

Arthur Peacock turned to LeCarre.

'Detective?'

'I don't see why not,' said LeCarre. 'As long as we all move to the dining room together and stay there until the group decides to retire.'

Pest screamed in delight. If the group relaxed, LeCarre supposed, the killer might relax. Then could come their slip-up and LeCarre would be there to pounce. As long as he kept his wits about him, this could bring about the moment he caught the murderer.


The group moved to the dining room, dragged the giant banquet table to the wall and turned it on its side, leaving a makeshift dance floor in the centre of the room. Seth Tuckerton made his way to the minstrels' gallery. They all laughed when it was discovered that the technologically inept Patricia Beresford had somehow connected her phone to the Bluetooth sound system.

'Honestly, I hate the thing!' she said, holding her phone. 'In my day we wrote each other letters!'

After a little bit of fiddling, Seth played his first song. Although the word 'song' would be an undue compliment in LeCarre's ears. To him it was just a dirge. No verse, no chorus, just a series of rapid bleeps. It wasn't that LeCarre had a problem with contemporary music. Some of the younger artists were very talented. Michael Bublé, for example. He could hold a tune. But this? This wasn't music at all. The only people who enjoyed it were on drugs.

If this 'music' wasn't hitting the spot for Detective Roger LeCarre, then the same could most certainly not be said for the Duchess of Totnes. Cynthia Pest was gyrating in frantic pleasure, shuffling feet, flailing arms. LeCarre was no fool. He'd shut down enough Redruth raves to know what he was looking at.

Cynthia Pest was under the influence ... *of drugs*.

There was no doubt about it. She was as high as the

Burj Khalifa, which at 2,722 feet is the tallest building in the world. Under normal circumstances, LeCarre would be searching her right now and looking to charge her with possession. But these weren't normal circumstances. There was a bigger picture to be considered, as big as the three-hundred-year-old oil painting hanging on the oak-panelled wall. Pest was still a suspect for murder. The longer LeCarre allowed her to continue in this state, the more likely she'd be to give herself away. And if she wasn't the murderer? And LeCarre caused a scene by arresting her? Well then, that too could cause a problem, shifting LeCarre's attention and allowing the actual murderer to kill again. No. He'd leave her be. There were bigger fish to fry. *Murderer fish.*

To LeCarre's surprise, Patricia Beresford had allowed the rhythm to grab hold of her body. She, Pest and Angela Peacock had formed a little trio in the centre of the room, dancing for each other's benefit. At one stage Patricia Beresford grabbed hold of Cynthia Pest's face and spoke intently to her, staring into her eyes. LeCarre had felt that there was a dislike between the Duchess and Beresford, but that appeared to be gone. A bond was forming between them all. Arthur Peacock, standing at the side, gently nodding his head. That, LeCarre suspected, was the closest Arthur Peacock had got to letting his hair down in many a year.

Angela Peacock saw LeCarre and gestured for him to join the girls. Dancing wasn't something Roger LeCarre tended to do, especially to this sort of electronic nonsense. If Seth Tuckerton changed things up and stuck on some Eric Clapton unplugged, then maybe he'd think about moving his hips a little. LeCarre politely held his hand up, declining Angela's invitation.

'Not your sort of music, Detective?' shouted Angela across the dance floor.

'Not really,' he replied.

Angela spoke to Cynthia Pest, who then walked purposefully over to LeCarre.

'What song do you want to hear, Detective?' said Pest.

'Oh. Nothing,' he said. 'I'm fine. You carry on.'

'Detective LeCarre. We're going to get you dancing. It's my mission. Seth has pretty much every song on Earth at his fingertips. What song do you want to hear? What would get you dancing?'

Despite LeCarre's reluctance to play along, the fact was that he had an answer. There was a song to get him dancing. The greatest song ever recorded. Why not? Anything was better than the abuse his ears were taking right now.

He told Cynthia, and she headed to the small stairway just outside the room, that led to the minstrels' gallery. Seconds later, he saw her on the balcony, hugging Seth Tuckerton and passing the request on.

From the first note, LeCarre was glad he'd answered Cynthia Pest's question. The song took him back immediately. To his youth, to a time when the future was an open highway, when the only crime he had to worry about was the crime of the sun coming up and ending another glorious night on the Devon party scene. Every muscle in LeCarre's body was inspired to move, inhaling the earthy guitar, soaking up every last ounce of rhythmic cool, every bar. Even Arthur Peacock couldn't help but make his way to the centre of the dance floor and join in. That was the power of the song. That's what it could do to you. LeCarre looked from Angela, to Patricia, to Arthur, to Cynthia and Seth, arms aloft on the balcony. Every one of them, humming along, every one of them, enjoying every second of the BBC snooker theme tune.

Then everything changed. The song was two minutes and thirty seconds long. Not a bad way to spend the last two minutes and thirty seconds of your life. After the final note, everyone in the room turned to each other with huge beaming smiles. Patricia Beresford clapped her hands together once in delight.

The next sound was a thud after Cynthia Pest tumbled down from above and onto the hardwood floor. And looking down on her from the balcony was the man who'd surely pushed her to her death – Seth Tuckerton.

# TWENTY-SEVEN

The tragic death of Cynthia Pest came with one silver lining. They had their man. LeCarre had started the day as a prisoner but he ended it as a jailer, throwing Seth Tuckerton into the cupboard. Tuckerton cried as Roger LeCarre and Arthur Peacock led him there, tearful, pathetic, bubbles expanding from his drugged-up nostrils.

'Be a man, at least,' said LeCarre. 'You were man enough to kill three people.'

'I didn't! I couldn't kill Cynthia! I loved her!'

'You think I've never met a man who killed a woman he claimed to love?' said LeCarre. '*I've met eleven.* I'm guessing you wanted Cynthia for a wife; she wanted you for a bit of rough. You wanted her for yourself but she was holding out for a prince. It doesn't matter now, anyway. I don't care why you did it. We all saw what happened.'

'She jumped!' said Tuckerton.

'Cynthia Pest was a lot of things, Tuckerton. She was a duchess, she was a drug addict, she was a troubled young woman. But she was no Greg Rutherford, by which I mean the 2012 Olympic long jump champion. She was no jumper. Only one woman jumped to her death in this castle and her name was Rihanna Peacock, may she rest in peace.'

LeCarre slammed the door and locked it. He turned to Peacock, whose head was bowed in thoughts of his wife. LeCarre's own experience earlier on in the day had taught him that locking the door wouldn't be enough.

'Seal the exits.'

'Yes, sir,' said Peacock, who went to make sure that all trap doors were shut. Tuckerton wouldn't be leaving until LeCarre had arranged for Chief Superintendent Beverley Chang to arrive with a police van.

LeCarre crouched down and spoke through the door.

'I know why you killed Cynthia Pest. I know why you killed Eli Quartz. Why did you kill the Bishop of Exeter, Seth?'

'I didn't.'

'Seth, the game's up. Two murders, three murders, you're

never leaving prison. You might as well tell the truth. Why did you kill the Bishop? And how did you go about framing me? You're a smart man, Seth Tuckerton. Shame, and I'm sorry to be the one to tell you this, Seth, HMP Exeter doesn't have a pub quiz team. Come on, tell me, how did you frame me?'

'Frame you? I'm in here, ain't I? Didn't do a good job if I did,' said Seth.

'No, not for Cynthia. I guess that was a crime of passion. The others – they were premeditated. You managed to get me holding the tusk and you managed to get me holding the gun. Very smart. How did you do it?'

'I didn't,' said Seth. 'I don't know what you're talking about. I wasn't even here. I was in the outhouse when all that was happening, wasn't I?'

'You disappoint me, Seth. Don't you know how this is supposed to work? I catch the killer, and then the killer and I talk it all through. Wrap it all up. Show each other some grudging respect. There's only one thing I hate more than crime, Seth, and that's bad manners. Not filling in all the blanks for me is very bad manners indeed.'

'You want bad manners, I'll give you bad manners,' said Seth. 'Fuck off.'

'Actually, if you were listening properly you'd know that I specifically said I *didn't* want bad manners,' said LeCarre.

LeCarre shook his head. What was the world coming to? Seth Tuckerton was the worst kind of killer – a killer who swore.

'Your room's ready for you, Detective,' said Arthur Peacock. 'I think we could all do with some sleep.'

LeCarre stood up.

'What about Anthony Little-Hope? He's out there somewhere?'

'We won't find him now,' said Peacock. 'It's too dark. I'm sorry to say, I think he may be another victim of this terrible weekend.'

LeCarre nodded.

'You're right, Peacock. You and I, we'll look when it's light.'

'Absolutely, sir.'

LeCarre began his ascent up the grand staircase to his bedroom. The bedroom he'd never got to sleep in the night before. He was ready. Now he could rest.

'Oh, Detective?'

'Yes, Peacock.'

'Thank you. For everything you've done.'

LeCarre looked at the floor. Had he really done anything? He hadn't caught Tuckerton. Tuckerton had effectively handed himself in by throwing Cynthia Pest off the balcony in front of everyone. It was nice to be thanked though. Coppers didn't get thanked much. Teachers – they got thanked. When Destiny was at primary school, they'd always, at the insistence of Carrie, got the teacher a Terry's Chocolate Orange or whatever at Christmas. Police didn't get Terry's Chocolate Oranges to say thank you. All police got was a pittance of a salary, the odd black eye and total immunity from prosecution if a suspect died in their custody.

'I've left a little something in your room,' said Peacock. 'Hope you enjoy it.'

'Thank you, Peacock. Goodnight.'

'Goodnight, sir.'


LeCarre closed the door behind him and looked at the luxurious four-poster bed. Catch a killer, go to sleep. That's the way it had always tended to go for Detective Roger LeCarre. It made for an incredibly unhealthy sleep pattern. Sometimes he'd find himself praying for a murder to happen in Exeter, just so that he could apprehend the killer and get some rest.

*He could rest now.*

On the dresser, LeCarre noticed a generous slice of chocolate cake, with a note.

*A small token of our appreciation.*

*Arthur Peacock*

A nice gesture. Not that he had the appetite for cake right now. He had the appetite for rest. Or maybe a KitKat Chunky.

He climbed into the bed and gently placed his head on the pillow, like the valuable asset it was. Was it a deserved rest? An unwelcome thought. Something didn't feel right.

Looking back at him was a face – that framed photo on the bedside table, from all those chapters ago. Do you remember? I think it was at the end of Chapter Three.

He knew the face. But from where? Not television, no. He'd seen it somewhere else, in person. He'd been face to face with that face. He'd *interrogated* that face. It was a young, freckled face, underneath cropped, light brown hair. Eighteen? Nineteen? The young man was giving a shy, reluctant, closed-mouth smile. His eyes seemed to be looking at the person behind the camera. They seemed to say, 'Leave me alone'. Although eyes obviously can't talk. Mouths do that.

In LeCarre's giant mind was a database of everyone he'd ever met: every cop he'd ever worked with; every friend he'd ever made on his travels across the two counties; every woman he'd ever slept with; Will Carling, the former England rugby captain, whom he'd met at a BBQ in 2013. One category dominated all others – criminals. He'd met far too many criminals and this man, the young man in the picture, he fell into that category. LeCarre knew it. He just couldn't think who. There'd been so many.

*Why would a criminal's picture be framed and placed on a bedside table at Powderham Castle?*

The eyes. What colour were they? LeCarre couldn't tell. He didn't know that colour's name but he'd seen that colour somewhere before. He'd seen it this weekend. They were ... they were the same colour as Angela Peacock's eyes.

Just then, there was a knock at the door.

# TWENTY-EIGHT

Woman, the finest creature on Earth, with the possible exception of the snow leopard. The first woman was Eve. That's what the Bible would have you believe. The earliest known skeleton found resembling a woman was uncovered in Ethiopia and is thought to be 3.2 million years old. This woman was bipedal, upright and believed to have dwelled in trees. Over hundreds of thousands of years women, along with their male counterparts, made their way to the ground and became what we know today as *Homo sapiens*. With each generation women have developed and become, like with each new model of the iPhone or the Kia Ceed, better versions of themselves. Angela Peacock was the culmination of 3.2 million years of evolution. Womanhood's newest iteration, and its finest example yet.

Standing before Detective Roger LeCarre, in his doorway, was one of the most beautiful sights in the world. It was as if Machu Picchu itself had knocked on his door. Machu Picchu, but with breasts.

'I'm sorry, Detective. I hope I didn't wake you.'

'No, no.'

LeCarre hadn't even taken off his tuxedo.

'Can I come in?'

'Certainly.'

The plan had been for them all to stay safely locked inside their rooms, away from each other, away from the killer. The plan was no longer needed. The killer was in the cupboard.

'Please, take a seat,' said LeCarre.

Angela Peacock rested her elegant behind on an armchair, cruelly hiding it from view. Her massive symmetrical eyes looked at LeCarre. He spied the room's small bar.

'Can I get you a drink?' he said.

'Yes. Thank you. Tia Maria, please.'

LeCarre poured her a large Tia Maria, and one for himself. They each took a sip, letting the dark coffee liqueur hit their taste buds and then absorb into their blood via their stomachs and small intestines. It was a moment before either of them spoke.

'I needed that,' said Angela Peacock.

'Long day,' said LeCarre. 'Although obviously all days are technically exactly twenty-four hours.'

'You did an incredible thing today, Detective.'

'Did I?'

It didn't feel like he had. It was less than an hour since Cynthia Pest had fallen to her death, on his watch. Anthony Little-Hope was missing, presumed dead. Exeter, not that it knew it yet, was without a bishop and Devon was without an earl. LeCarre had merely witnessed a series of terrible events. He hadn't prevented them.

'You saved Patricia Beresford's life.'

Oh yes. He'd forgotten about that. It's not often that you save a life and forget about it before the end of the day. Crazy times.

'Yes, I suppose I did,' he said, raising his glass. 'Let's drink to that.'

They both downed their drinks and LeCarre poured them two more Tia Marias. Inside their bodies a battle was commencing between the stimulant coffee and the depressant alcohol, like the battle between good and evil that had been fought in the castle all day. This was the first time it had felt like good might have the upper hand.

Angela Peacock rotated her body, which is to say she

turned a bit, and picked up the framed picture on LeCarre's bedside table. The one of the unidentified young man. She looked at it and a tear formed in her right eye – or her left eye if you were looking at it from LeCarre's point of view.

'Who is he?' said LeCarre.

'I didn't know my father had done this.'

'Done what?' said LeCarre.

'Put his picture here. He obviously wanted you to see it,' said Angela.

'Me? Why? Who is it?'

'You really don't remember, do you?'

LeCarre took the picture from Angela and looked at it again. He searched his massive database but kept coming up blank. It was just too big.

'That's Peter,' said Angela.

'Peter Peacock?' said LeCarre. 'Your brother?'

Angela nodded.

'Your father told me he'd died,' said LeCarre. 'I'm so sorry.'

'He's not dead, Detective,' said Angela. 'Although some-times I think he may as well be.'

'He's not? But your father ... he said he'd gone.'

'Gone,' said Angela. 'Not dead.'

LeCarre kicked himself for making an assumption.

Arthur had just told LeCarre about Angela's dead mother. When he'd said that Peter had 'gone', LeCarre had jumped to a conclusion – the wrong one.

'Then where is he?' said LeCarre.

'Prison,' said Angela. 'HMP Exeter. *You put him there.*'

# TWENTY-NINE

Peter Peacock. LeCarre had forgotten him, tucked him away in a secret passageway in his giant mind, but now it all came flooding back.

Peter Peacock was a good kid, they'd all said. His headteacher, his mother Rihanna Peacock, even Chief Superintendent Beverley Chang had told LeCarre to go easy on him.

'Don't call the CPS,' she'd said. 'Which is an acronym for the Crown Prosecution Service. Just give him a caution.'

'A caution? And what am I supposed to tell the CEO of Superdrug when he calls me up and asks why a packet of Wrigley's Extra chewing gum has gone missing from one of his stores and no one's been held accountable? We both know he did it, Beverley. His breath stinks of spearmint.'

'It's just a packet of gum,' Chang had said.

LeCarre had nearly thrown up in his mouth. Just a packet of gum? LeCarre had been chasing Peacock for weeks. It wasn't one packet of gum. It was ten, fifteen, twenty of them. Every Saturday Peacock had been there, in the Guildhall Shopping Centre, in Superdrug, hidden from CCTV view, nabbing his preferred choice of chewy confectionary. And now Chang wanted to give him a slap on the wrist? Not even the face. The wrist! The wrist is such an odd place to slap someone.

This was the problem, as LeCarre saw it. Crime was crime. You let some kid off lightly for some supposedly minor offence and they thought they could do it again and again. It would only be a matter of time before Peter Peacock moved on to more serious crime – drug dealing, tax evasion . . . murder. This was a matter of life and death. If they let Peter Peacock, a habitual thief, back into the community before he was twenty-five, he'd be a killer. LeCarre was certain of it. He made sure that Peacock was convicted for each individual instance of stealing: that meant time in prison. A long time. Ten years in total because that's exactly how sentencing works.

LeCarre didn't mind if other officers looked on him as being too tough. There was no such thing as too tough. The way he saw it, by putting Peter Peacock away he was stopping a future murderer in his tracks – he was saving lives.

Except he hadn't. The horrible truth was becoming clear. He'd done the exact opposite.

Peter Peacock's imprisonment had led Rihanna Peacock to jump to her death. No Grey Lady had pushed her. She'd, in effect, been pushed by Detective Roger LeCarre and his determination to lock away her son. Deep down, Arthur Peacock knew that Rihanna had jumped and he blamed one man – Detective Roger LeCarre.

Just as his family life fell apart, his work life did too. Eli Quartz arrived. To Arthur Peacock, Eli Quartz represented the modern world, a world he despised. The world that, he felt, had taken away his son and then his wife. Eli Quartz did not belong at Powderham Castle. By killing Quartz, the modern world's most famous global advocate, Arthur Peacock could express his rage and, by framing Roger LeCarre, he could kill two birds with one stone – something LeCarre had actually done once when skimming pebbles on the River Exe. Peter Peacock, as Arthur saw it, had been unfairly imprisoned by Detective Roger LeCarre. Why not give Detective Roger LeCarre a taste of his own medicine? Why not get *him* sent to prison?

When Eli Quartz asked Arthur Peacock to put together a

small guest list of local luminaries for his celebratory castle-warming, Peacock devised his plan, a plan that didn't just include the demise of Quartz and LeCarre. When a man's world falls apart to such a degree, he grows mad at God; you can't kill God but you can kill the next best thing – the Bishop of Exeter.

Detective Roger LeCarre took the framed photo from Angela and looked at it again.

'Peter Peacock. I remember him now.'

Roger and Angela looked at each other. Angela now knew that Roger knew what her father had done. Roger knew that Angela knew. Angela knew that Roger knew that Angela knew. Roger knew that Angela knew that Roger knew that Angela knew. They knew.

'Why did he try to kill Patricia Beresford?' asked LeCarre. 'And why did he kill Cynthia Pest? How the devil did he do it? Were you involved in the murders?'

Angela placed her hand on Roger's knee.

'I promise to tell you everything. But there's something I want you to do for me first.'

'And what's that, Miss Peacock?'

'Make love to me.'

All the blood drained from LeCarre's face. Why? It had somewhere else to be. Downstairs there was an innocent man locked in a cupboard. Elsewhere in the castle was a butcherous butler. Suddenly, all of that was peripheral. Detective Roger LeCarre was a cerebral man, a caring man, an intelligent man, a complex man but most of all, he was a man and *no man* could resist the charms of Angela Peacock. Unless they were Alan Carr or Graham Norton or one of the other many gays with whom LeCarre had absolutely no problem at all.

Angela stood up and undressed herself, revealing the wonders that hid behind her servant's clothes, wonders that were exactly to Roger LeCarre's tastes. It was as if a five-foot eight-inch cognisant KitKat Chunky had developed the ability to unwrap itself. He sat on the edge of the four-poster bed and admired her. A beguiling clavicle above not just one, but two perfect breasts. A circular navel at the lower centre of an excellent abdomen. An effortless mane of naturally blonde hair stretched down her back like a hairy waterfall finishing roughly four inches above where her anus was likely to be.

'You're beautiful,' said LeCarre. 'You're stunning ... you're ... you're ... '

He picked up a thesaurus from the small pile of books on the bedside table.

'You're winsome. You're prepossessing. You're appealing. You're smashing. You're decorative. You're pulchritudinous.'

Angela Peacock put her pulchritudinous finger to LeCarre's lips.

'Stop talking. Stop talking and take me.'

Angela was taking control, just like the Egyptian President Gamal Abdel Nasser had taken control of the Suez Canal in 1956. The difference was that, unlike the British and French governments of 1956, LeCarre was happy for Angela to do so.

Angela lay back on LeCarre's bed and he realised that he'd only ever seen her vertical. She looked even better horizontal. LeCarre could only imagine how good she'd look diagonal. She was as pretty as a professional picture. LeCarre proceeded to kiss every square inch of her twenty-seven-year-old body, which took about forty-five minutes. It could have got a little dull if Angela hadn't thoughtfully suggested that they put on a podcast. LeCarre grabbed his Huawei P30 Pro and played an episode of the excellent historical documentary series *Battleground* about the Falklands War. As they learned about Margaret Thatcher's military task force's mission to the Falklands, LeCarre sent his *own* task force – a task force comprised of his hungry tongue and lips – to Angela's arms. Then her legs. Then her belly. Then her other parts.

\*

The episode finished at the same time as LeCarre. He looked up.

'How was that?' he said.

'Fascinating,' said Angela.

LeCarre was ready. Ready to entwine his own body with hers, ready to envelop her, ready to initiate her in the powers of his considerable manhood. But first, she had something to say.

'Wait. I'd like to return the favour.'

Angela went about stripping LeCarre. Was she intending on kissing every square inch of him? This was a double-edged sword. On the one hand, with his body being larger, with more surface area to cover, they were looking at at least another hour before actual penetrative sex; on the other hand, it would give them a chance to listen to the next episode of *Battleground*, which would be covering the retaking of South Georgia.

Then Angela picked up the slice of cake, the one left for LeCarre by her father.

'Let's have some fun,' she said, and began to smear it all over LeCarre's body. Wow. Food play. Roger hadn't done that in years. He and Carrie had spontaneously decided to try it one Valentine's Day but all they could find in the fridge was some leftover spaghetti carbonara. In the end,

they'd agreed that although they didn't regret the incident, they couldn't see it becoming a regular part of their sex life. Chocolate cake, though? This felt right, this felt exciting, this felt . . . LeCarre couldn't help but say the words out loud.

'This feels tremendously erotic,' he said.

Angela went about her work with frenzied enthusiasm. She began at LeCarre's ankle and ran her tongue all the way to his handsome knee via his shin. Then she did the same with his other shin, devouring every last drop of chocolate.

It was when she got to his thighs that LeCarre realised something was wrong. Very wrong. She looked up at him and suddenly all her playful eroticism had been replaced by something else – panic.

'What's wrong?' said LeCarre. 'Is it my legs? Are they too muscular?'

'The cake!' strained Angela.

'The cake?' said LeCarre. 'Too dry?'

Angela Peacock could barely get out the next two words – her final two words.

'It's poisoned!'


Detective Roger LeCarre had a rule: every year, acquire a new experience, do something you've never done before. One year it was wind surfing. Another year, it was

snowboarding. Another, it was to read a book by a woman. Just a few days into January and LeCarre had already managed to find this year's new experience – attempt CPR while naked and covered from head to toe in poisoned chocolate cake.

'No! Come back to me! We haven't even had sex yet! Come back to me!'

LeCarre felt as if he saw Angela Peacock's soul leave her body. It was a beautiful soul. Absolutely stunning. Pulchritudinous, one might say.

Killed by her own father. Like Marvin Gaye but via the medium of chocolate cake. But, of course, the chocolate cake was meant for LeCarre. Arthur Peacock had been gunning for him, or caking, to be more accurate. Framing LeCarre had failed, so now Peacock wanted him dead. Well, he'd failed at that too, but now LeCarre, standing over her, sure as shit looked like he'd killed Angela.

It's incredible, thought LeCarre, how one minute someone can be licking chocolate icing from your shins, and the next minute they can be dead.

'But I just saw him this morning!' people would often say when LeCarre broke the news that their loved one was dead. Really, when you thought about it, it was a nonsensical way of looking at things. That was the nature of life

243

and death. There was no easing from one realm to another. No mid-state between the two. It's a binary. You're alive and then you're dead. Angela Peacock was dead. Just like Eli Quartz. Just like the Bishop of Exeter. Just like Cynthia Pest. Just like any pretence that this had been in any way a successful castle-warming party. Just like Professor Anthony Little-Hope? Only time would tell.

LeCarre had to strategise. He looked at his phone. Still no signal. If he could elicit the help of Seth Tuckerton and Patricia Beresford, the only two other survivors, then they could surely apprehend Arthur – get him in the cupboard, let him think about what he'd done. But the Arthur Peacock that LeCarre would next face would not be the Arthur Peacock of before. He would now be a man who'd killed his own daughter, and knew it. Such a man would either crumble into a pathetic heap or, as LeCarre feared, direct his grief into violent rage. There was no telling how difficult *that* man might be to control.

LeCarre took a shower, soaped off the cake and prepared for the coming storm. As the water tumbled from above and down upon his cakey body he thought through the case and formulated a theory. It was if he was washing away not just the poisoned cake, but the confusion of the day.

He was clearer now. Then he got dressed. Not back in his tuxedo. No. That was the outfit of another man, a fictional man – James Bond. Detective Roger LeCarre was far from fictional and yet he had his own iconic uniform. Luckily, he'd brought it with him. Leather jacket, brown brogues, light blue wrinkle-free shirt, top three buttons undone.

LeCarre felt like a protagonist entering the final few chapters of a novel. He felt ready. Ready to end the story once and for all.

# THIRTY

Detective Roger LeCarre left the room quietly. It was vital that he wasn't heard. He had a theory to test and Powderham Castle was his laboratory. He made his way down the stairs without a sound. It was a skill he'd learned during the Great Tunnock's Binge of 2014. To his shame, that year LeCarre had developed an addiction to Tunnock's Teacakes. He found himself getting through in excess of two dozen a day.

Carrie and some of the lads from the force had staged an intervention and told LeCarre that his gluttony had to stop. Teacakes weren't just ruining his life. They were ruining the lives of those who loved him too.

So he told them he'd stop, told them he'd beat the demon teacake, he'd knock it on the head. But he didn't. He wasn't ready to. Not yet. He found himself a hiding place behind the carrier bags, just beside the gas meter, and every night, for three months, as soon as Carrie drifted off to sleep, he crept downstairs and scoffed delicious chocolate and marshmallow into his ravenous mouth.

Incredibly, even as his weight increased, his ability to creep downstairs undetected improved. It was that skill he used now in Powderham Castle. Gliding down the decadent stairway, making his way to the music room and to the trap door where he hoped he'd get his answer.

Having cleverly charged his Huawei P30 Pro while it was playing the Falklands podcast that accompanied his foreplay, he was able to use its torch function to find his way through the house. The trap door was in front of the fireplace, just beside where Eli Quartz had met his ugly fate.

Seth Tuckerton was still in the cupboard. Arthur Peacock had been tasked with sealing all of the trap doors to keep him there. This one, he'd dragged a chaise longue on top of. LeCarre just had to lift one end of the furniture and pivot it a few degrees. Gently, carefully, placing it back down so as not to be heard. Unfortunately for LeCarre, he set it down on his own foot and found himself letting out an involuntary yelp. He froze. The house was silent. As far as LeCarre could tell his yelp had gone unheard. Everyone was asleep. *Most of them because they were dead.*

A gentle push to the trap door caused it to spring up a little so that LeCarre could open it fully. He lay flat down on his stomach. The last time he'd done that, he'd been exploring Angela Peacock's body. Now he was exploring the space below the floorboards. He hung his head into the cavity and shone his torch in all directions.

*And there it was.*

The answer to the question he'd been asking for more than twenty-four hours now.

How was Eli Quartz murdered?

That morning LeCarre had climbed through that very crawl space and not found it. But then, he hadn't been looking for it. He'd only been searching for a way out. If he'd moved just a few more inches, past the trap door, he'd have seen it. Well, at least he had his answer now. Like a cheating pub quiz participant with a smart phone.

LeCarre pulled himself up and rested on his knees on the floor of the music room.

The ringing in his ears came before he felt the pain on the back of his head. Both came courtesy of the same blow. A blow that came from Arthur Peacock, who stood over LeCarre now, a cricket bat in his hand. LeCarre rolled over, flat on his back, and looked up to see Peacock preparing to

met the Peacocks for the first time. Now one Peacock was dead and one was as good as, for now.

LeCarre opened the door. All that time inside and now the freezing cold was battering his face. The snow had stopped falling. Now it was just the cold, cold wind attacking him like some kind of giant angry ghost. He touched the back of his head. It was starting to swell.

He could see down the long driveway that led to the world outside Powderham Castle. If only it led to the past. That way LeCarre could have arrived prepared. *No one could have prepared for this.* Although if LeCarre were honest with himself, he could have thought to bring a toothbrush. His breath stank.

The driveway was dark. LeCarre could just about make out the outline of some trees and the giant gates. Little else. But then he saw a colour in the distance. Blue. Blue could mean any number of things – a football team, a feeling, an internationally renowned performance art collective known as the Blue Man Group. To LeCarre it meant one thing and one thing only. It meant home. It meant the police.

Flashing blue. A siren. A squad car was passing by. The Devon and Cornwall Police were still out there, doing their jobs. The world where LeCarre belonged still existed. Of course it did; it was within touching distance, although obviously not literally because the driveway was seriously lengthy and LeCarre's arms weren't that long. But just as quickly as the squad car came, it went away. So be it. LeCarre now knew what he needed. Backup. Peacock could wake soon. LeCarre could probably get him in the cupboard but then what? They were still cut off with no communications. Wait it out? No. They'd waited too long. People kept dying. LeCarre needed his brothers and sisters in arms, he needed the Devon and Cornwall police force.

That squad car. You didn't just pass through parts of Devon like this. It must have been making a house call. LeCarre's bones, his blood, his D and C Police blood, his blue blood, told him so. A burglary perhaps. Or a domestic. Something in the village of Kenton, just beyond the castle's grounds.

Could he walk to the village? The snow was so deep. The giant gates would most likely be locked. Getting over them was an impossibility. The same went for getting around them with the dense shrubbery. There were some footprints. Little-Hope's? He was probably out there somewhere, frozen to death.

The Belvedere Tower. If LeCarre could get there and

ring the bell, then that would sound the alarm. If he could find the strength, then he could end it. He had to get to the tower before they left.

LeCarre ran. If you could call it running. Wading through the deep snow was like trying to push a shopping trolley across a beach. Progress was slow. His only blessing was that that meant progress would be slow for Arthur Peacock too.

Fifty yards from the castle, LeCarre saw a body face down on the ground. He shone his phone's torch towards it as he got closer. Red hair. Anthony Little-Hope.

Red hair. Red back.

*Blood red.*

A bullet wound between Little-Hope's shoulder blades.

LeCarre turned back to the castle. A window was ajar on the first floor. The perfect place from which to shoot someone in the back.

LeCarre went back to running. He had to get to the tower. He had to ring that bell.

He shone the torch ahead of him. A narrow country lane, branches arching over it. And somewhere, somewhere in the distance, a glimpse of the Belvedere. LeCarre was already exhausted but he had a long way to go. It was at that moment that he reached down inside his own body (metaphorically), pulled out his own soul (metaphorically) and looked at it (metaphorically).

'Don't stop. Keep moving,' he metaphorically said to his own soul before carefully putting it back inside his body.

He was a shark now. If he stopped moving, he'd die. Was that a fact? He was sure he'd heard it somewhere but he couldn't stop to check ... *because he'd die.*

Every step was a struggle. But that was what it meant to be Roger LeCarre. People didn't understand what it was like for a forty-something-year-old man with a mortgage in the West Country. Every day was a struggle. But you kept moving. It's what you did. Move or die.

The closer he got to the tower, the faster he moved. The end was in sight. One foot after the other. Keep moving. He could still only see the top of the Belvedere; the bottom was obscured by a group of trees. As LeCarre got nearer the picture became clearer. The Belvedere Tower was at the top of a small but steep, almost vertical, hill. Whatever strength LeCarre had left would be required to make his way to the top.

Boots, crampons and an ice axe – that's what he needed. What he had was his leather jacket and brown brogues. Never in his life had he so wanted to stumble upon an open branch of Millets. But there was no Millets here.

There was just a tower and Detective Roger LeCarre had to get there.

He started scrabbling his way up the incline, using his hands as well as his frozen feet, the snow having penetrated his brogues. For every few feet he gained, he'd fall back a couple. Progress was slow but it was progress nonetheless. The calorific excesses of Christmas were being worked off in double time.

Perhaps he was tired, or perhaps it was the thought that he was so nearly at the finish line. LeCarre fell and this time he couldn't regain any grip. His handsome body slid all the way down to the bottom.

Cold. So cold. As cold as snow. Because it was snow, although Detective Roger LeCarre didn't know that yet because he was slowly regaining consciousness.

He pulled his face out of the snow, turned and saw Arthur Peacock running towards him. He'd recovered from LeCarre's cricket bat blow, the bastard. That didn't look like a sixty-year-old butler running through the snow. Peacock's strides were long and high and fast.

*Was he?*

Yes. He was.

Peacock was wearing a pair of Eli Quartz's jumping

boots. The ones LeCarre had seen in Quartz's study. Each stride was a leap, springing off the ground with apparent ease. LeCarre had no time at all. He started scrabbling up the hill again. This time it was easier. A murderer on his back was just the shot of adrenaline he needed. Quite the motivator. Maybe if he had a murderer on his back all the time, he'd get a lot more done. Maybe everyone should have a murderer on their back. It could give the Devon economy just the productivity boost it needed.

LeCarre reached the top of the hill. *His* Everest but roughly five hundred times smaller. At the front of the tower were two large barn-style doors. LeCarre pushed at them. Locked.

He ran around the Gothic tower's base. It was essentially a folly, about the size of a windmill, with three turreted corners at the top. LeCarre found a smaller door at the other side. He didn't even need to push it. The door was open.

The tower looked like no one had entered it for years. Inside were rusty tools, piles of damp boxes, a half-filled-in Euro 96 wall chart. All LeCarre's effort depended on the bell working. His heart sank at the creeping realisation that that was by no means guaranteed.

He ran up the spiral staircase. Had anyone run up those stairs with such urgency in centuries? The last man to do so might well have been wearing armour. LeCarre had no armour, just a gritty determination to end things and get back to his wife, child and Waterpik water flosser.

At the top was a cold, empty, stone-walled room. Empty but for a bell at the centre.

LeCarre grabbed the single rope and pulled it. And again. And again.

The sound of the bell echoed around the room and rang out over the fields that surrounded him. It was a confident sound that would be heard for miles. Any copper worth their salt would follow that noise.

LeCarre looked out of an open window. Arthur Peacock had reached the bottom of the steep hill. LeCarre rang the bell again.

'You bastard!' shouted Peacock.

'Right back at you, Peacock,' LeCarre shouted back in quite a cool way.

Their voices carried easily in the cold, crisp air.

The boots that had helped Peacock so much had become his problem. The springs could get no purchase on the snowy hill. The harder he tried, the harder he fell.

'It's over, Peacock,' said LeCarre. 'My colleagues will be here soon and they'll be taking you to jail. Sit back and enjoy the fresh air. The next fresh air you'll be getting will be in the HMP Exeter exercise yard.'

LeCarre was about to begin his speech. It was a speech he'd given a thousand times before and he'd give a thousand times again. It was the speech all coppers gave when they finally caught the murderer, the one in which they methodically explained how the murderer did it and how the copper had caught them. LeCarre loved giving that speech. It was his reward for doing his job.

He leaned against the window frame and looked down on the pathetic Peacock. He was going to enjoy this.

*But then . . .*

'Hello, Detective.'

LeCarre turned.

Seth Tuckerton was standing in front of him. LeCarre looked at his feet. No snow, no nothing. He didn't even look like he'd broken into a sweat.

# THIRTY-ONE

'You're just in time, Seth,' said LeCarre. 'I was about to give my speech.'

'Yes, I thought you might be,' said Tuckerton.

'How did you get here, Seth? Don't you have a cupboard to be in?'

'Arthur sealed all the trap doors but for one,' said Tuckerton. 'The one at the bottom of this tower.'

'You crawled all the way here?' said LeCarre. 'That's a lot of crawling, Seth.'

'Not for me it ain't. I've been crawling through those passageways all my life.'

'Yes,' said LeCarre, 'I thought as much. You were crawling last night, weren't you?'

'Can you speak up a bit?' shouted Peacock from the

bottom of the hill. 'Only, if this is the speech, I'd quite like to hear it.'

'Sure,' said LeCarre. 'This pertains to you both. Arthur, you killed Eli Quartz. You killed the Bishop of Exeter, you killed Professor Anthony Little-Hope and just a short while ago, you accidentally killed your own daughter. But you didn't do it by yourself. You had some help.'

LeCarre looked at Seth Tuckerton.

'Last night,' said LeCarre, 'before the mayhem began, before people started dying, we heard rats under the floorboards. Except they weren't rats, were they, Seth? They were you. You were getting into position.'

The blood drained from Tuckerton's face, like brine draining from a tin of tuna.

'You both wanted the new Earl of Devon dead, so you hatched a plan. Eli Quartz was murdered by an elephant tusk, but not the one I was holding. That's the thing about elephants, Seth. They have two tusks. And you had the other one, under the floorboards. When the thunder came and the lights went out, that was your cue. It was then that you handed Arthur the second tusk, with your tobacco-stained hands. That makes you an accessory, and I'm not talking about the kind of accessory you can buy at Claire's, formerly known as Claire's Accessories. You're no hair clip. You're an accessory to murder.

'Peacock, you did the deed. You stabbed Quartz with the second tusk, you brutally used all of your five feet eight inches to plunge it into his chest. Then you, Seth, you transferred some of Quartz's blood onto the tip of the tusk I was holding to make me look like the murderer. Peacock couldn't do it because everyone would see the blood on his hands. Well, I can see the blood on your hands now, Peacock. I can see it clear as day.

'Seth, of course, you weren't the only accessory. Angela Peacock, she had a role to play. You see, this whole plan depended on a storm, a clap of thunder and the lights going out. You knew there was a snowstorm coming, but nature was never going to tell you exactly when and if the thunder would arrive. That's where Patricia Beresford and her extensive library of BBC sound effects came in. You knew she had them on her phone. Angela Peacock used her Bluetooth to connect them to the speakers and when the moment came, when I was holding the tusk – of course you knew Eli Quartz would bring out the tusk. It was his pride and joy. You knew he'd want to show it off and you knew he'd ask for a man's help holding it. Anthony Little-Hope was too weedy, the Bishop of Exeter was, well, he was a bishop, so Quartz was always going to ask me – that was when Angela played the thunder sound effect from Beresford's phone and that was when Angela shut off the fuse box. She was standing right by it. So when the lights went out, the plan went into action, and a very well-executed plan it was too. Almost as well executed as the three men you killed.

'Next to die was the Bishop of Exeter. This one was all your work, Arthur.'

LeCarre looked down at Arthur Peacock, still standing at the bottom of the hill, listening intently.

'You were the man who handed me the gun, right before Eli Quartz's funeral. Little did I know you were handing me my goddamn arse. That gun was rigged. "You can rig this baby up to pretty much anything." That's what Eli Quartz had said about his remote control. Turns out that "pretty much anything" includes guns. You rigged the 12-gauge, didn't you, Arthur, and the second I had it pointed towards the Bishop, that's when you activated it. My finger was nowhere near the trigger but that made no difference. You fired the gun and you did it from the other side of the chapel. Yes, your plan depended entirely on my pointing the gun at the Bishop at one stage or another. But, heck, I guess it worked. You were angry at God so you killed God's Devon spokesperson. Not nice, Arthur, not nice at all.

'Not everything was going to plan. You kept framing me but I kept getting out. That's when you decided I had to die. You baked a poisoned cake and Patricia Beresford nearly died when she stole a bite in the kitchen. Then, later on, Anthony Little-Hope made a run for the tower. You didn't want him ringing that bell. Not before you'd killed me. You also didn't like the idea of him and his History department getting Powderham Castle. So you shot him in the back from an upstairs window as he made his way through the snow. You killed three men, Arthur, and you'll rot in prison for it.

'Then there was Cynthia Pest. That's the only death this weekend you had nothing to do with.'

LeCarre turned back to Seth.

'I didn't push her. I swear I didn't,' said Tuckerton.

'I know you didn't, Seth. Not literally, anyway. But you might as well have done. You gave her drugs. That's why she got in touch with you and you know it. Yes, she wanted sex but she knew you'd probably have some cocaine in the outhouse and that's what she really needed. There was only one problem. What do drugs do? They make people think they can fly. That's fine when they're on the ground. But once she was up in the minstrels' gallery, it was only a matter of time before she jumped to her death. You'll have to live with that, Seth.'

'I didn't give her drugs, I swear I didn't.'

'You're already going to prison, Seth, for your part in Quartz's murder. Why lie now?'

Seth said it quieter now, beaten.

'I didn't give her drugs.'

'Save it for the judge,' said LeCarre before turning to Arthur Peacock again, who seemed to know what was coming.

'Eli Quartz, the Bishop, Anthony Little-Hope, Cynthia Pest. Four people who didn't have to die. But there was one more, wasn't there, Arthur?'

'Don't,' whimpered Peacock. 'Please don't.'

'One day you're going to have to face up to what you did, Arthur. Whether it's in this life or the next. Baking a poisoned cake is dangerous. You nearly killed the county's finest radio actress and you very nearly killed me. The trouble is, Arthur, poison and cake are a dangerous recipe, especially when two people are wildly attracted to each other. Arthur, when you baked that cake, did it not even occur to you that your daughter might end up licking it off my body? It should have done. You'll go to prison for the men you killed, Arthur. But you'll punish yourself for Angela. I know you will.'

Arthur Peacock was a broken man. He reached inside his coat and pulled out a gun, the same gun that had killed the Bishop of Exeter and Anthony Little-Hope. LeCarre and Tuckerton hit the ground, waiting for a bullet to come their way. But it didn't. Instead, Arthur Peacock placed the gun in his mouth and fired a bullet into his own head. He fell back into the snow, the blood slowly expanding out, in a way that would look particularly good in an aerial shot in the film of this book.

LeCarre took a second to contemplate the butler's demise. Then another second to think about how Butler's Demise would be a good name for a racehorse. That was one second too many, because it was in that second that Seth Tuckerton made a run for him.

Five hundred years of Devon heft, all contained within Tuckerton's agricultural body, were powering towards LeCarre, trying to push him out of the window. Tuckerton was like a turbo-charged combine harvester headed straight for him. The problem for Seth Tuckerton was that Detective Roger LeCarre wasn't ready to be harvested. LeCarre's mind rattled through his roller deck of martial arts moves and landed upon the right one. Using Tuckerton's force against him, LeCarre crouched down and flung him against the stone wall. Tuckerton got up, turned and ran for LeCarre again. Same outcome. Straight against the wall.

'We can do this all night, Seth,' said LeCarre.

Tuckerton let out a visceral, animal cry. His massive fist struck LeCarre in his Devon gut. LeCarre grabbed the back of Tuckerton's head, pushed it down and kneed him in the face. Tuckerton spat out a tooth and smiled at LeCarre, revealing his bloodied mouth. LeCarre thought about giving him a roundhouse kick to the face but decided his jeans were too tight. There was no need. He had this under control.

'Give up, Seth. I play squash. You don't stand a chance,' said LeCarre.

Another animal cry from Seth. It seemed to contain all the rural angst and frustration of a millennia of Tuckertons. One more charge towards LeCarre, like an angered bull running at a matador. LeCarre's skills were too great. He crouched down again and flung Tuckerton over his shoulder and, this time, out of the open window behind him.

A few hours before the snow might have softened the fall. Not now. It was frozen hard. Tuckerton died when he hit the ground. More death. LeCarre was the only one left.

*Or so he thought.*

A Land Rover was making its way up the hill and when it arrived at the foot of the tower, a head popped out of the window and a familiar voice called out to LeCarre. A very familiar voice indeed.

'Can I help at all?' said Patricia Beresford.

LeCarre's shoulders drooped. It was over.

He looked out over Devon. *His* county. It had never looked so beautiful. And in the distance, something was making its way towards him.

A Devon and Cornwall police helicopter and seated beside the pilot, LeCarre could just make out the distinctive outline of Chief Superintendent Beverley Chang.

# EPILOGUE

Detective Roger LeCarre looked down at the moules marinière and let the garlic-and-parsley-scented vapour fill his handsome nostrils. He forked a mussel from its shell and ate it. The mussel tasted good. He'd earned this.

Three months ago, on that January night, when Beverley Chang had arrived by helicopter, he'd fallen to his manly knees in relief. The bell had worked. A young copper, PC Daniel Ginola, had been in the squad car. He'd been called out to investigate a new piece of graffiti on the village's vicarage wall.

The roads were clear; they'd been clear since that morning. Peacock had lied. But the driveway to the castle was too treacherous for Ginola's simple panda car to traverse. And anyway, the gate was locked. All there was were some footprints. The footprints left by Peacock, who'd walked down to the gate to collect the pizzas from the delivery-man. That was when Ginola radioed command. When Chang had heard that a bell was ringing at Powderham Castle she knew something was seriously wrong and got straight in the helicopter. LeCarre was in trouble and she had to get there. He was her best copper, after all, her trustiest cog in the wheel that was the Devon and Cornwall police force.

What she had found was a bloodbath. No one liked a Saturday night bath more than Beverley Chang, but not *this* kind of bath. She'd told LeCarre to take the week off to recover. Of course, he was in on Monday morning. That was the kind of man he was, although when he'd realised that the snooker was on telly that week, he'd asked if the offer still stood and went back home to watch it.

LeCarre took a quick glance around Café Rouge and then at his companion for the evening, none other than Patricia Beresford.

'Very good, Ms Beresford,' he said. 'An excellent recommendation.'

'I told you, Detective. Best mussels this side of the Channel,' said Beresford.

Now that he'd tasted how the other half lived, would he

return? He could take Carrie here. What would be so bad about coming to Café Rouge once in a while? As a treat.

No. This place was for the likes of Patricia Beresford. The likes of Eli Quartz. Detective Roger LeCarre didn't belong here. He didn't belong at Powderham Castle either. He belonged out there, on the partially cobbled streets, amongst the dirt and the grime.

'I'm so glad you agreed to meet, Ms Beresford,' said LeCarre.

'I wouldn't have missed it for the world, Detective. I must say, it's a pleasure to see you under different circumstances. That was quite the weekend.'

'Yes, it was,' said LeCarre, taking a frite (which is French for chip) and placing it in his mouth for immediate mastication. 'How are you finding life after *Jam on Top*, Ms Beresford?'

'Oh, it's marvellous,' said Beresford. 'I should have quit years ago. Do you know, I think that programme was holding me back. I'm getting so many opportunities now. I've just started rehearsing a production of *The Pirates of Penzance* at the Plymouth Theatre Royal, I already have a pantomime booked in for Christmas and,' Beresford leaned in and went into a stage whisper, 'don't tell anyone, but there's talk of a guest role on *Doctors*.'

'You sound very busy,' said LeCarre.

'Oh, it's nothing, really,' said Beresford with false modesty. 'You said there was something you wanted to talk to me about. I'm simply dying to know.'

LeCarre placed down his cutlery and wiped his mouth.

'My word, Detective,' said Beresford. 'Your face has gone awfully serious.'

'Seth Tuckerton didn't kill Cynthia Pest.'

Now it was Patricia Beresford's turn to let go of her cutlery. She looked at LeCarre in astonishment.

'What? But we all saw him push her.'

'No, we didn't. What we saw was Cynthia Pest jump,' said LeCarre.

'Really?' said Beresford.

'Surprised, Ms Beresford?' said LeCarre. 'Or are you acting surprised? You're very good at *acting*, aren't you, Ms Beresford?'

'What?' Beresford was flustered. 'What on earth do you mean?'

'Cynthia Pest jumped. I thought it was because of the drugs in her system. That was, until the toxicology report came back. Turns out there were no drugs in the Duchess's system. No drugs at all. She stayed clean the whole weekend. She was just high on music, high on this crazy thing we call life. But why did she jump? The fact is, Ms Beresford, Cynthia Pest didn't have a choice in the matter. But you did.'

'This is getting absurd,' said Beresford. 'Where's the waiter? I think we should get the bill. *Garçon!*'

'Seth Tuckerton wasn't much more than a *garçon* when you met him, was he, Patricia? A teenager? But that didn't stop you falling in love with him.'

A tear formed in Patricia Beresford's astonished eye. This was no performance. That tear came from the heart. Although, obviously biologically it came from a tear duct.

'You said you were a nanny once, when you were trying to make it as an actress. I managed to get hold of your work history. It's all available. Most things are, when you're a detective who knows where to look. Turns out you only ever had one nannying job, for one summer. At Powderham Castle. You looked after the Tenterhook kids but it was the young Seth Tuckerton who caught your attention. You were already far too old for him, but that didn't stop you having a fling. Then Cynthia Pest showed up. She was closer to Tuckerton in age. They had more in common. It broke your heart. We've watched your tragic love life over the years, Ms Beresford, in the Devon press. The racing car drivers, the property magnates, the Exeter City players. None of them

272

ever seemed to work out. Why? Because you were always thinking of Seth Tuckerton.

'"Well, you better get here quick. Please don't do this to me. I'm tired of living a lie. I love you." Those were the words the Bishop and I overheard you saying, on your own, in the state dining room. I thought you were rehearsing something but no writer could write anything that good, that raw. Those words were very real. You were using the internal landline to talk to Seth Tuckerton out in the out-house. Then, when he arrived with Cynthia Pest, you knew what had happened. You knew they'd been making love. You tried to cover it up and you did well, you're a brilliant actress, but deep down you were heartbroken.

'Nannying wasn't the only job you told us that you'd done in the past. You were also a stage hypnotist. Don't get any ideas, by the way, Ms Beresford. You can't hypnotise me. I'm immune to hypnotism. Unfortunately for the Duchess of Totnes, she was not. I saw you speaking intently to Cynthia Pest just before she went up to the balcony. You were hypnotising her, weren't you, Ms Beresford? You were jacked up on jealousy and Cynthia Pest was the reason why. So she had to die. When the BBC snooker theme tune finished, you clapped your hands. I didn't realise it at the time, but I do now. *That was the trigger. The cue for her to jump.*

'It might as well have been a bullet directed at her regal brain. You killed her and for that you will have to pay the price. I'm afraid Plymouth won't be seeing you in *The Pirates of Penzance*. The next production you do will be for a drama society *in prison*.'

Patricia Beresford pushed the bowl of moules marinière away from her. She no longer had the stomach for it.

'I thought I'd got away with it,' she said.

'You nearly did,' said LeCarre. 'I can see why you fell in love with Seth Tuckerton. He's a fine young man.'

LeCarre looked to the entrance of Café Rouge. Seth Tuckerton was still on crutches, but getting better every day. The physiotherapy was difficult but Seth was used to hard labour. He made his way to their table.

'Take a seat, Seth,' said LeCarre.

'Evening,' said Tuckerton, casually.

'Seth!' said Beresford. 'I thought you were ...'

'Dead?' said LeCarre. 'I did too ...'

'Oh, you've already eaten?' said Tuckerton. 'I was gonna ...'

'Hang on, Seth,' said LeCarre. 'I'm just tying up all the loose ends. Yes, we all thought Seth was dead. He fell from quite a height but although the snow was hard, it was soft enough for him to live. Just about. While you were giving a statement to Chang, *a statement full of lies*, a medic was reviving Seth. The Royal Devon and Exeter worked their magic and, well, here he is.'

'Oh Seth!' said Beresford. 'I'm so glad you're alive!'

'Bitch,' said Tuckerton.

'Yes, Seth and I have something in common,' said LeCarre. 'We don't take kindly to murderers. It took me a while to see it, though. You see, I thought Seth helped Arthur Peacock murder Eli Quartz, but I was wrong. Seth, I hope you don't mind me saying this – Seth's not the brightest man in Devon. No place for him on my pub quiz team, I'm afraid. He thought he was just helping Quartz out with a demonstration. That's what Peacock had told him. He had no idea that when he handed up that tusk, he was enabling a murder. Daubing my tusk with blood – Peacock whispered in his ear and asked him to do that. It was dark, it was frantic, I doubt Seth had any idea what was going on. We don't have enough to charge him and do you know what? I don't want to. There's been enough suffering. Besides, I wouldn't want to get on the wrong side of the next Earl of Devon, would I, Seth?'

Beresford furrowed her brow in womanly confusion.

'It's ancient Devon law, Ms Beresford. I happen to be a bit of an expert in the law. When the Earl of Devon dies, if there are no living relatives but one single person lives in the grounds of Powderham Castle, then that person shall inherit the title and Powderham itself. It's a shame it never worked out between the two of you. I'm sure you would have made an excellent countess, Patricia. Instead, you'll have to make do with being an excellent inmate.'

LeCarre was pleased with himself. It was a good line to end on. Chang arrived to take Beresford away. Patricia left screaming, dramatic until the end. Another criminal off the streets, thanks to Detective Roger LeCarre. He poured Seth a glass of wine and looked at the menu. A dessert? LeCarre felt like he deserved it. But nothing took his fancy. No. Not tonight. He could always grab a KitKat Chunky on the way home.